Amateur Theatricals

Anne Louise Bannon

HH
Healcroft House, Publishers
Altadena, California

ISBN: 978-1-948616-39-3

Library of Congress Control Number: 2024913962

Copyright © 2024 by Anne Louise Bannon

Healcroft House, Publishers, Altadena, California, United States of America

All rights reserved.

No portion of this book may be reproduced in any form without written permission from the publisher or author, except as permitted by U.S. copyright law.

Contents

Acknowledgements	V
Dedication	VII
1. January 5, 1987	1
2. January 6, 1987	17
3. January 8, 1987	31
4. January 9 - 11, 1987	45
5. January 12 - 13, 1987	59
6. January 14 - 16, 1987	73
7. January 17 - 20, 1987	89
8. January 22 - 29, 1987	101
9. February 4 - 6, 1987	129
10. February 8 - 12, 1987	143
11. February 13 - 23, 1987	159
12. February 24 - 26, 1987	173
13. February 27 - March 7, 1987	185

14.	March 9 - 13, 1987	203
15.	March 18 - 21, 1987	217
16.	March 22 - 24, 1987	233
17.	April 15, 1987	237
Coming Soon		243
Thank You for Reading		245
Other books by Anne Louise Bannon		247
Connect with Anne Louise Bannon		251
About Anne Louise Bannon		253

Acknowledgements

Writing is largely a solitary endeavor, which is great because I love being alone.

That being said, one does have to come up for air and social contact every now and then. I am profoundly grateful for my different communities. They have provided support, kindness, solid and much-needed laughter, and often inspiration.

So I'd like to thank the Transition Pasadena Repair Café for building a community out to help the world one repair at a time.

Thanks go to my virtual communities, the Lady Sings the Clues Author Pod and the Blackbird Writers.

And, finally, my own little family. My long-suffering husband, Michael Holland, and my daughter Corrie Klarner (best TMI pal ever).

Dedication

When I first wrote Amateur Theatricals, I was finishing up my master's degree at California State University, Fullerton. At the time, the Operation Quickline series was a respite – someplace I could hide from the pressures of directing a thesis production and then writing that project up.

When I did the re-write of this book, the series had again become a respite, this time from the COVID pandemic and all the fears that generated. But this book also became a fond remembrance of the time I spent in the Theatre Department.

So to all the faculty, staff, and students I knew – thank you all.

January 5, 1987

This was it. After three full months of strategizing and preparation, Sid pulled the UHaul truck into the driveway of a modest ranch-style house of yellow stucco and red bricks on the bottom. It was barely nine a.m.

"Well." Sid turned off the engine. "It's show-time."

I smiled at him, then looked at our son, Nick, who was sitting between us, grinning nervously.

For the next however many months, we would be the Devereaux family, teaching and going to school at Collins State University in Collins, Kansas, a small town somewhere between Topeka and Kansas City. Sid and I originally planned to go undercover as a pair of older students finally able to take time off from their careers to finish their educations. But then, a history professor had unexpectedly gotten sick, and we and our coordinating team had decided that Sid would come in as a visiting professor hoping to land a permanent job. I'd take classes as a theatre student. Nick would go to the university's special school run by the education department.

Going undercover is scary. Sid and I had agonized over bringing our thirteen, almost fourteen-year-old, son. After all, what parents in their right minds would want to risk their kid's neck in an undercover counter-espionage investigation? We sure as heck didn't. But that is the problem Sid and I have as members of Operation Quickline, a shadow agency under the auspices of the FBI that is so secret that mostly only its members know it exists. Nick hated the idea of us being gone for so long and reminded us he was just going to be worried and upset the whole time, which would not help with our cover at home. He also pointed out, quite rightly, that having a kid around would make us look a lot less suspicious. Then there was the reality that Sid and I didn't want to be away from him that long, either.

We had been training Nick for the past eighteen months since we'd taken custody of him in the summer of 1985. It was almost shocking how good he was at things like tailing suspects without getting made and getting information out of people. So, Sid and I had made the difficult decision to include him in the operation.

We got out of the truck. Sid had seen to lightening his and Nick's hair and cutting Nick's hair short. He also cut and darkened mine. Sid wore his glasses and Nick wore contact lenses, which both really hated. The two look so much alike, it's almost eerie, with bright blue eyes and cleft chins. They're both very nearsighted, although Sid usually wears contacts and Nick wears glasses. However, the idea was to change our appearances just in case our cover got blown.

There was a small Toyota sedan hitched to the rental truck, and we all pulled suitcases out of the trunk. Nick started running to the door of the house.

"Careful, son!" I yelped. "It's probably icy."

The snow was piled at least three feet deep in the front yard, with slightly higher berms on the yard's edges. Nick slid, and I rolled my eyes.

Still, we got inside the house with no more problems. Sid winced. At home, we are independently wealthy and live in a large house in Beverly Hills. Here, the front door opened onto a small living room. A hall on the left led to three bedrooms and the one bathroom in the place. To the right of the living room was a dining area and small kitchen with appliances that looked like they'd been there since the 'Fifties. At the back of the kitchen was a door that led to a dank basement which held the washer and dryer and the house heater and fuel bin.

"It's not bad for an associate's salary," I told Sid.

"I know. It's just one of those details," he grumbled.

When you're undercover, it's those details that make all the difference. Technically, Sid's title was visiting associate professor, but that also meant a lean salary and we'd decided it was better to live within those means than our own.

"At least, we're not poor," I said.

"No. I've been poor. This is not poor. It's just not rich." Sid much preferred being rich, and I couldn't blame him.

Our first job was to double check for listening devices, of which there were none, and to install trip wires on all the windows and doors on the place, so that we'd know if anyone had come in besides us or if we'd been bugged. All three of us carried small bug finders that were linked to the trip wires and could alert us to a listening device. Mine looked like a face powder compact. Sid's and Nick's looked like part of a key chain.

Our next job was to unload the rental truck and return it. After that, we'd contact our coordinating team, then get some food in the house. Sid and I had gone over all the likely chores and had divvied them up between the three of us. Nick was not enthused. At home, we have a housekeeper, Conchetta Ramirez, who was currently taking care of our dog and three cats. Here, if the toilet was going to be kept clean, we would have to do it. Or, rather, that one was Nick's job, along with the rest of the bathroom and his room. I had dusting and laundry. Sid was going to take on cooking, thank God, [I wasn't going to let you cook. - SEH] and keeping the place swept and vacuumed. We all were responsible for cleaning up after meals, and there was no dishwasher. I was glad that Nick was going to get some basic training in life skills, but was not happy about the dusting. I hate housework.

Fortunately, it didn't take that long to unload the furniture, the boxes of books and kitchen equipment, and other things we'd decided were essential. The upright piano was the toughest thing to get inside, but since it had wheels on its base, it turned out to be a lot easier to move than you might think.

At the truck rental center, I made the phone call to the coordinating team, and we agreed to meet at a local diner for dinner. Now, one reality of working in a top-secret organization is that no one is supposed to know who you are, and the vast majority of the folks we work with do not know our real names or where we actually live. That doesn't mean we don't recognize people. If you're passing secrets to the same people over and over again, you get to know what they look like. Or if you've worked with them before on a case. You may not know their real names, but you recognize them.

I started laughing quietly as Sid, Nick, and I walked into the diner where our meeting was. Sid chuckled as well. Nick sighed.

"What are you laughing for?" he asked softly.

"It's a long story," said Sid.

Nick sighed loudly, but seemed to understand.

The other couple waiting for us looked puzzled, at first. We didn't look the same way we had the last time the couple had seen us, although we'd been told they knew we'd have our son with us. They were sitting in a booth in the back corner of the room. He was a medium-sized, balding man with wire-rimmed glasses. She was a petite brunette who blinked a lot.

As we got closer, his eyes opened wide, then he nudged her and whispered in her ear. They both got up quickly, and he held out his hand.

"Dr. Charles Devereaux, it's good to see you," he said, shaking Sid's hand.

She blinked and hugged me. "Linda, I am so happy to see you."

"Son," Sid pushed our boy in front of him. "This is Dr. Randall and Dr. Irene Garrett. This is our son, Ryan Devereaux."

Randall and Irene Garrett were not the names we'd known the couple by, nor were Charles and Linda Devereaux the names we'd used at that time. Nick shook hands with Irene first.

"He's such a cutie!" Irene said to me as Nick shook Randall's hand.

"Nice to meet you guys." Nick's smile was polite, but he was not thrilled with being called a cutie. Well, he was a little over a month shy of his fourteenth birthday and already as tall as me.

We settled into the booth, forcing Nick to the outside seat with his back to the door. Irene almost had her back to the room, but Randall, Sid, and I all made sure we could see the whole restaurant from where we sat. Irene leaned over to me.

"We heard you two got married," she said softly.

"Yeah. Last year." I smiled.

"Where was the boy when you were in Wisconsin with us?"

"With his mom. I adopted him last year."

Irene blinked and giggled. "Linda, I can't tell you how happy this makes me that we're going to be working together. I meant it when I said I hoped we'd see each other again."

"I know." Grinning, I nodded. "I was hoping I'd see you again, too, but we don't have a lot of control over things like that."

"Well, Randall asked specifically for you guys when the situation came up. Only they said they were giving us Big Red/Little Red, and Randall said they had quite a reputation."

I chuckled. "Apparently, we do. I don't get it."

"We had no idea that those were your code names."

I rolled my eyes. "They didn't tell us you were the coordinating team, which is, of course, one of the bigger pains in the butt about this business." I grinned. "But I'm glad."

The waitress came by and got our order and we chit-chatted until the food came. Irene taught communications, although it was out of the social sciences department rather than the marketing or journalism departments. Randall smiled at her happily, but you could tell his mind was somewhere else. Irene explained that after we'd known them, Randall had gone back to teaching chemistry (he'd been teaching history in Wisconsin) and had discovered it was his first love after all. Nick, who loves chemistry, looked like he wanted to talk to Randall about it, but then our dinners showed up.

"We've got a lot to go over this evening," Randall said, snapped back to life. "We're establishing that Linda and Irene are old friends from your undergrad days at University of Wisconsin, Madison."

"And obviously, our cover is that we've been married a lot longer than we have," said Sid, doing some math in his head. "So, I guess that's where Linda and I met before we moved to Los Angeles."

"That works," I said, mentally making a note of that.

"As far as the rest of our team is concerned," Sid continued. "We have Nancy and David Lemon. Nancy's got math/sciences as an engineering grad student. David is taking the music department going for his master's in music."

"Got that," said Randall.

Sid nodded. "Karen Crombie is working in the financial aid department."

"That will get her a lot of access to the students and their records," said Irene.

"Her husband, LeShawn Pile, is taking on a master's in journalism." Sid looked over at me and I nodded.

"Exactly." Randall nodded eagerly. "We made them all grad students, except for Crombie, so that they can take your section of Research Techniques and Resources."

"That's good." Sid swallowed. He wasn't showing it, but he was pretty nervous about that class. "How did you set that one up?"

Randall laughed. "Nobody wants to teach it, but it's required for first quarter grad students, no matter what their discipline."

Sid glanced at me. "Not my strong suit."

"You'll be fine," Randall said. "We'll work on the course outlines this week and for your other history sections. Those are basic first year stuff, so that won't be a problem. You'll be lead on the investigation since you have a visible reason for knowing all of us. Linda, of course, is right in the middle of it all."

"About that," I said. "How am I in the middle of it?"

"Because of Fedor Andreyevich," Randall said. "You'll know him as Earnest Kaspar. He's the directing professor. Well, he's an MFA, so if you want to call him a professor, that's up to you."

MFA is Master of Fine Arts, which is based more on practical work rather than the theory and academic focus of a regular master's degree. It does, however, entitle one teaching at a university to call oneself a professor, no matter what Randall said. But then, Randall is a dyed-in-the-wool academic with PhDs in both chemistry and history.

"He's the KGB agent running the finishing school," I said, suddenly understanding.

"That's him," Irene said, her eyes blinking even faster than normal.

Randall sighed deeply. "I should have known those assholes from The Company had something else up their sleeve when they set Irene and me up here after we went into Witness Protection."

The Company is the CIA. Randall had been recruited as a young man and was a known operative. At least, he was by his real name. Assuming I'd known him as his real name on that case in Wisconsin, where Sid and I had met him and Irene.

Randall rolled his eyes. "I spotted the finishing school operation almost as soon as I stepped on campus. I had a kid who was flunking his training in one of my classes, and another who was almost there, but not quite."

Randall was talking about a program the Soviets had to finish training KGB agents to blend into American society. Our side didn't know how many such programs they had, but we knew about a few of them. Oddly enough, instead of rooting the programs out, we pretended we didn't know. That way, our side could keep an eye on the KGB agents, keep them away from the critical stuff, and even feed them some bad intel every so often.

"The problem is, we've lost four of the students since last summer," Randall continued.

"Four?" Sid asked. "I thought there were only three."

Irene sighed. "We lost number four right before Christmas."

"We're probably looking for some rogue agent on our side," Randall said. "The problem is, Irene and I are the only people on our side on campus that we know of. All the other shadow agencies say they've accounted for all of their personnel."

"Could it be one of the other KGB agents?" I asked.

"Possibly." Randall shrugged. "But why? There is absolutely nothing for the KGB to gain by killing their own people."

"True." Sid shook his head. "It might seem crass, but why are we worried about someone killing KGB agents? I would think The Company would be handing out medals."

Irene snorted. "If it had been their idea, they would."

"The problem with rogues is that you can't control them," Randall said. "This guy may be going after the other side now, but he could turn against our own as easily as not."

"And we know how much The Company loves giving up control," I sighed.

Randall shook his head. "Even if it is one of the KGB moles taking out his colleagues, we've got a significant problem. Local law enforcement won't be that effective at finding the killer because they can't know about the victims being moles, and we can't have them finding out about the moles because that would give away that we know about the finishing school."

"Any chance we can look at the police reports?" I asked. "It would probably help to stay on top of what the cops are doing about the murders."

Irene pulled an envelope from her bag and handed it to me. "We've got the initial reports on all four. It's just tough getting in and out of the police station all the time and if we have to keep asking the FBI to get the reports, then the local cops are going to wonder."

Sid glanced at me. "We should be able to do something about that."

"There are three remaining students. I still have contact with Clayton Webster," Randall said. "He's a chem major and in a couple of my classes. Rita Kominski is an electrical engineering student. And Greg Grimsbacher is studying journalism."

"Well, that sounds like everything," Sid said, finishing his chef's salad.

Nick and I had already grabbed the ham slices Sid had set aside.

"We do need a visible reason for Charles and me to be spending some extended time together this week," Randall said.

"Do you have a lab?" Nick asked suddenly.

He'd been so good about staying quiet during the meeting, something that was incredibly difficult for him, as hyperactive as he was. So, Sid and I just smiled at the interruption indulgently.

"Of course," Randall said. "I'm a chemist."

"Can Dad and I meet in your lab? I'd like to see a real chem lab."

Sid grinned. "Our boy is a budding chemist."

"I don't know about that," I said, trying to look severely at my son. "Things in your lab at home have a nasty habit of going bang."

Nick attempted some chagrin as he laughed. "I really like blowing things up."

"I know a lot of folks who do, too." Randall laughed deeply, as if he was one of them. "I'm afraid I can't let you do too much of that. But I think we can keep you occupied while your father and I are working."

"Keep in mind, son, you have school tomorrow," Sid said.

"I understand you enrolled him at the university test school," Randall said.

"We thought we'd give it a shot." Sid grinned again at our son. "Ryan is pretty gifted and has ADHD. It has not been easy keeping him challenged and settled."

Nick/Ryan shrugged his shoulders. "I don't mean to get into trouble. I just do."

Randall and Irene both laughed, and Sid and I shook our heads.

Randall smiled again at Sid. "Most of the kids at the test school are children of faculty, so the school encourages all of the faculty to offer enrichment programs. I've got about four kids from the school who are my Lab Rats. They come over after school every day. I can take on another. Gifted education is one thing we're noted for at Collins. Ryan should do well there. You can pick him up at two-thirty and bring him right over to the lab."

"One other thing." Sid winced. "Exercise facilities? We'll need to keep up on our workouts and we can't go running in the snow."

Irene and Randall looked puzzled for a second, then Irene nodded.

"The exercise center is on the first floor of the Physical Education building," she said. "It's open for everyone, including family of faculty." She rolled her eyes. "Some of the faculty wives use it as their base of operations. In fact, Linda, there's a little wives' club. They are the most petty, insipid idiots ever spawned. Randall and I were at some big faculty bash the year we started here, and they wanted me to join their group since my husband was the new chemistry professor. I pointed out that I was also a professor in communications studies. That didn't count.

Women faculty don't have husbands who are also faculty. One of them wanted to know why I would endanger Randall's chances of getting tenure by trying to teach here as well."

Randall waved for the check. "Oh, I almost forgot. We're down the street from your house, about four houses down. Practically that whole subdivision houses faculty. Sebastian Lovegood, the college president, owns your place, and ours, too, come to think of it."

"That's good to know," said Sid.

"More important." Irene suddenly blinked faster. "It's the faculty wives again. You're across the street and a house down from the Howards. Raylene is the wives' ringleader, and she is a real stickler for property maintenance."

Sid shrugged. "So? It's winter. There isn't much we can do with snow on the ground."

"That's exactly the problem." Irene shuddered. "It doesn't matter that you're renting. As a resident, you are responsible for snow removal on the sidewalk in front of your place. You have twenty-four hours after the snow stops to clear your sidewalk or you will get a citation. Raylene knows to the second the time the last flake fell, and she will call the city at twenty-four hours and one minute afterward."

"What if it snows and we're away for the weekend?" I asked.

"According to Raylene, that's no excuse." Irene laughed. "However, most of us renters notify the management company when we head out of town during snow weather. It just costs to have them take care of the removal. And to be honest, almost everyone on Faculty Row screws up once or twice a season and the city Public Works will almost always waive the fine because they know Raylene and can't stand her. Still, it's a major hassle to get the fine waived, nor does anyone want to get on Raylene's bad side."

"Why not?" Sid asked.

"Her best friend is Isabel Lovegood," Irene said. "As in the college president's wife. Also, Raylene's husband is Dr. Carl Howard, chair of the history department, and Dr. Lovegood's particular pet."

"Howard is a genius at fundraising," Randall said, blinking back to life after fading out for a minute. "He's also a suspect, but not much of one. He was the classic oxymoron in Korea."

Sid laughed. "Army intelligence?"

"And he exemplifies the oxymoronic part of it." Randall shook his head. "He's not a complete idiot, except where Raylene's concerned, and he tends toward a Bible Belt mentality."

"Now, honey." Irene put her hand on Randall's. "His scholarship is solid, never mind his religious inclinations. Even you admit that."

The waitress brought the check by, and Randall insisted on picking it up. Sid, Nick, and I then drove over to the supermarket Irene had recommended. The interesting thing about Collins, Kansas, was that the entire town seemed to exist to serve the state university. As we later found out, that wasn't that far off from the truth. There was little in the town that dated back before the 1950s, when the university was built. There were lots of apartment buildings for students. Even the test school that the university ran was the primary school for the area.

At the supermarket, Sid was not thrilled with the produce selection, but did not complain. We both sighed when we saw the total at the check stand. Nick's appetite had backed off a little since he'd begun his big growth spurt the summer before, but he still ate a lot. Given that I do, too, food was going to be a major part of our budget. When we finally got back to the house, I got out of the car to open the garage door. Flurries of snow drifted through the air. Sid pulled in, but Nick ran outside to look at the snow in wonder.

"Awesome!" he yelped. "It's snowing!"

Nick had been skiing with Sid and me often enough that snowfall wasn't a complete novelty. Still, neither he nor Sid had really lived with snow. Sid had been mostly raised in San Francisco and then had moved to Beverly Hills. Nick had been raised by his mother and grandmother in Sunnyvale, a suburb of San Jose (which was a little ways south of San Francisco). Me, I had grown up in the mountain region of South Lake Tahoe and knew from living with snow.

"We'll see how you feel about it snowing when we get up tomorrow," I said darkly.

Sid just sighed. Inside, the place was such a mess, we decided to put the police reports we had aside until we could get settled in and concentrate. It wasn't as though we'd be doing any active investigation right away. We had beds to assemble, first, and the boxes with the sheets in them found. All three of us were exhausted by that point and went to bed soon after.

January 6, 1987

The good part of our current cover was that there was a lot of room for culture shock. We were a nice little family from California. Of course, it would take some time to really fit in with even a university town like Collins, Kansas.

The downside, at least from Sid's and Nick's perspective, was that instead of our usual affluent lifestyle, we were living like more normal people. Okay, from my perspective, too. Compared to Sid, I am rather tight with money. But not having had to worry about how much money I had for a few years had left me a little on the spendthrift side. The problem was, I fell into my more fiscally conservative habits [Try miserly. - SEH] a lot faster than either Sid or Nick did.

It was still dark when we got up the next morning. The house was cold because I'd turned the thermostat down to save on heating bills. We'd gotten up extra early because Nick had to be at his new school at eight and Sid wanted to be sure we got a workout in. Little did he know what kind of workout awaited us. We'd kept an eye on the snow falling and it looked like it had stopped a little after ten, when Sid and I went to bed. There were a good several inches of it on the sidewalk and driveway when we opened the front door. Thank God, there were two snow shovels in the garage. I pulled them outside to see Sid walking through the snow to the side of the house.

"What's up?" I asked.

"The snow stopped at, what, ten?" he asked me softly.

"I think so."

He nodded to the side of the house. "Get a look at this."

There were the indentations of several footprints right under the window to Sid's and my bedroom. I noticed something else as we came around to the front of the house and the bedroom window on that side.

"Two different sets here." I pointed. "One that matches that other set and a second, really heavy boot, it looks like."

A police car pulled up on the street in front of the house and a lone officer got out.

"Good morning," he told us as he walked up the snowy driveway. "Sorry to come by so early, but we got a call last night about some screaming in your house."

Nick guffawed and his father and I glared at him.

"It wasn't like that," I said.

The officer chuckled. "The report says that there was some noise, but not indicative of anyone in trouble."

Sid shrugged. "We like sex. I'm just surprised that the noise carried outside. The house is pretty well insulated, and the windows are double-paned."

"According to the watch command, it wasn't that loud."

"Officer," I pointed to the two sets of tracks in front of the window. "Could one of these sets of footprints belong to one of your colleagues?"

The officer came over and squatted down over the tracks. "Yeah, that's one of our regulation boots."

"Do you know who the second set belongs to?" I asked.

"Can't say, but..." The officer glanced at the house next door.

Sid looked at him thoughtfully. "If the noise wasn't that bad and there's nothing going on that shouldn't be, why are you here?"

The officer laughed again and glanced again at the house next to ours. "Just letting your nosy neighbor see that we're following up on the call. You guys are new here, right?"

"We moved in just yesterday," said Sid.

"Okay. Well, not that it's a big deal, but there are a lot of really bored housewives on this street, so don't be surprised when you see us."

The officer sauntered back to his squad car and drove away.

"That will not be helpful," Sid grumbled.

"Nothing we can do about it." I shrugged.

I started in on the sidewalk, only to have my lower back explode in pain when I'd barely gotten three feet in.

Sid cursed. "You didn't."

"It's okay." I blinked back tears and tried to get the shovel under the next bit of snow.

"No, it's not." Sid waved at Nick. "Come on, son. This will be our workout this morning."

Nick took my shovel with the sigh of the truly beleaguered. I went inside the house and did several stretches, none of which helped much, then took a shower. The guys came in as I was blow-drying my hair and I warned them against going around with wet hair in freezing weather.

Sid put together breakfast while Nick was in our one shower. I ate, then listened to Sid curse as the hot water in the shower ran out. I had packed my super-sized Motrin tablets. The problem, as I looked at the boxes littering the kitchen and living room floors, was that I had no idea where the tablets were.

"You're lucky," Nick grumbled as he staggered into the kitchen.

"What do you mean?"

"Dad said you can't do any more shoveling."

I clenched my teeth. "Son, do you have any idea how much my back hurts right now?"

Nick's eyebrows rose, and he backed off. "Okay. Sorry."

Sid's mood was not great, but not nearly as bad as it could have been. He kissed me quickly as he came into the dining area, then piled fruit on his plate. Sid's preferred breakfast is fresh fruit salad, whole wheat toast, and prune juice. We'd been able to find whole wheat bread and prune juice. There hadn't been much fresh fruit at the supermarket besides apples, oranges, and bananas, and the bananas hadn't looked that good.

We got the Toyota sedan out of the garage and on the road in plenty of time to get Nick to the university school, officially known as the Evelyn Casey Education Center, by eight. Sid dropped both me and Nick off, then went to go to the provost's office to get himself signed in as a new faculty member and all the attendant paperwork done.

Dr. Schilling, the school principal, came out of her office just long enough to say hello to me and Nick, then passed us off to Ms. Westmore, a young woman with a filled-out build, brown hair, and hazel eyes that peered at us through very thick glasses.

She looked through the file folder in her hands. "We're going to have Ryan do the full battery of assessments with the teachers today." She looked up at me and smiled. "It's the usual protocol for new students. Mr. Clark has his open period now, as does Ms. Stillwell."

Ms. Westmore went through the list of all the teachers who would talk to Nick over the course of that school day, then sent Nick off with Mr. Clark.

"Now, we need to get your perspective," Ms. Westmore said. "Given Ryan's scores on his entrance exams, he is gifted, but his past grades don't seem to support that."

I sighed. "That's probably the ADHD."

Nick had been officially diagnosed that previous fall, thanks to his current teacher back home. The diagnosis had come as no surprise to anyone who knew Nick. The problem was that because Nick had come into Sid's and my lives so late - he was eleven at the time - and because his first mother had been rather difficult about sharing information with us before she died, we didn't know if Nick had been diagnosed earlier in his life. Nick said he didn't remember any tests, nor had he taken any medications.

"Ryan also gets bored a lot," I continued.

To my enormous relief, Ms. Westmore chuckled. "Just looking at his paperwork, that doesn't surprise me. Are you medicating?"

"No. Adaptive behaviors. My mother taught Ryan to knit, and that seems to soothe him."

Ms. Westmore grinned. "That's terrific. Knitting is great for kids."

"The other problem we've had is that while he's behind in history, geography, and English, he's way ahead of his classmates in math and science."

"That's interesting. Any discipline problems?"

That one really made me sigh. "Mostly impulsive behavior."

There was also Nick's problem with bullies. He hated them. He'd been bullied as a younger child. When he'd come to live with Sid and me, we'd started training him in self-defense right away because he'd need those skills to stay alive. But the training had also given him enough confidence to stand up to the bullies at his school, not only for himself, but for the younger children, too. He didn't start fights, by any stretch, but if a bully came after him or another, weaker kid, Nick could and would hit back.

I did not encourage this. However, the two times Nick had punched another kid, he'd been standing up against the bullies in question. The second time, the bully had been about to hurt a seventh-grade girl when Nick stepped in. Nick even let the bully hit him first before taking him out with punches to the belly and head. The bully's mom was not happy, given that her son had gotten the worst of the fracas, but she couldn't say much since her son had started the incident and had started plenty of others at the school.

I looked at Ms. Westmore, wondering if she'd understand that, and decided not to take the chance.

"Impulsive behavior," Ms. Westmore wrote down. "Well, that's no surprise with the ADHD." She smiled at me. "I'm sure Ryan will do well here. As I'm sure you know, the Evelyn Casey Education Center runs from pre-school through twelfth grade. Its mission is to educate children in a positive learning environment that helps each child develop his or her full potential and individuality. The reason we do such extensive assessments on each child is that students are not assigned to specific grade levels.

Instead, they are assigned to pods of similarly skilled students in each subject area. So, based on what you just told me, your son may work with high school age students in math, but perhaps sixth grade age in geography. It's also not unusual, especially with new students, for the child to be reassigned to a different pod as he or she adjusts to the new environment. We'll go over Ryan's assessments and discuss his education plan this afternoon. Can you be here at one-thirty?"

"Sure. Thanks."

I left and slid back into my parka, a dark green one that went down to my knees, and given the bite in the air that morning, I was glad I had it. I wasn't supposed to meet Sid until two-thirty over at Randall's lab office. I could have walked back to the house, it wasn't that far away, but I thought getting to know the campus a little better would be a good idea. Like many such schools, most of the buildings faced onto a quad, currently filled with snow and a couple students having a snowball fight. Four large buildings sat apart from the main complex. The first was the education building, which sat next to the Evelyn Casey Education Center, what most people referred to as the Test School. The buildings were connected through the basements by a tunnel. Both of those buildings were behind the Humanities Building and the student Commons and Bookstore.

The Physical Education building was across a snowy field from the Education Building. I wandered over there, picking my way slowly along the cleared walkway. My back was still hurting quite a lot. I hadn't found my pills, either, and I'd checked my monster of a purse. It was black leather, filled with pockets on the inside, but it was also pretty deep, and I carried a lot with me. I found the exercise center, and there were plenty of stationary bikes and treadmills, and the weight machines were nice and modern. The free weights section was huge, too. Lockers were available with a student ID, and I suddenly remembered that I needed to go back to the administration building and get mine.

I ate lunch in the Commons, and both regretted it and was grateful. The regret was because the food was pretty bad, and I was grateful that it would be little temptation. Eating lunch out was going to be a bit of a luxury, even at the Commons, given how tight our budget was.

I took a quick look around the Humanities building, where Sid would be teaching, but didn't see him. There was a covered bridge on the second floor to the Performing Arts building and I went there to look around, as well. It looked like the second floor was mostly given over to the Music Department. All the offices were there. A sign on the wall pointed up a staircase to the practice rooms and the Costume Warehouse. Downstairs was the Theater Department. The faculty and department offices were on the outside edge of the floor closest to the Humanities building. I found Kaspar's office, but it was dark, as were several of the others.

The back edge of the building was filled with two large dance studios, and across from the studios were two huge dressing and restrooms, one for the women and one for the men. The two main stages, the scene shop, and the costume shop were on the opposite side of the floor from the offices.

Across from the costume shop was a room that had been painted green and featured some of the ugliest, most broken down furniture I had ever seen. Two couches and three easy chairs were grouped facing each other in front of some gray cabinets with a counter and a sink that had probably not been washed in... I'm not sure I wanted to know. A small white fridge sat under the counter. I did not open it. There was also a small microwave oven on the counter, but again, I shuddered at the thought of using it. Closer to the door, in the back corner, a round table sat in the middle of four unmatching rickety chairs with plastic seats and backs and one with the seat but no back. I later learned that anything in that room was a leftover that even the scavengers in the scene shop had decreed unusable.

Just outside the door, several sheets of paper had been taped to the wall. Most were the usual announcements about classes and such. One announced auditions for Top Girls on January 14 and 15 in the Studio Theatre. Sid and I had seen the play in New York while on a case in 1983. A tall man with thinning gray hair and wire-rimmed glasses was busy taping a second notice to the wall. As I smiled at the Top Girls announcement, he looked over at me and smiled.

"Hello," he said in a soft, but cultured voice. "You look like you're new here."

"I am," I said. "I'm just checking things out before school starts next week."

"Ah. I'm Doctor Edgar Dorfmann. And you are...?"

"Linda Devereaux. Dorfmann? I think I have you for Voice and Diction this quarter."

He thought for a moment, then smiled. "I believe you do. Well, welcome to Collins." He pointed at the notice he'd just taped to the wall. "You will be required to audition, you know."

"Oh." I looked at the notice and couldn't help laughing. The auditions were the same nights as for Top Girls, but the play was Shakespeare's Richard III. "Ah-hah. The hatchet job on Grandpa's enemy."

Dorfmann laughed. "I haven't heard it put quite that way. But you are familiar with it?"

"So-so. I did my undergrad degree in English and managed to get through almost all of the plays."

"You're not a grad student." He looked at me, curious.

"Not yet. My husband is a visiting professor in history here, so until we know whether he'll be able to stay on, I'm taking undergrad pre-requisites before tackling the master's."

"I see." He lifted an eyebrow. "Well, I would recommend you find a good monologue by next Wednesday. Anything but 'Set down, set down.' You know every girl in the department will want to do that one."

The character of Anne was considered the female lead in Richard III, and her big monologue began "Set down, set down."

"I think I can find something." I nodded.

"Excellent." Dorfmann chuckled, then rolled his r's. "Brush up your Shakespeare!"

"And they'll all kowtow." I grinned, quoting the tune from Kiss Me, Kate.

He laughed outright, and I moved on. From there, I went on to the Administration Building and got my student ID, and then it was time to get back to the test school.

The assessments were pretty much what I expected. Nick would be in a pod with mostly fourteen- and fifteen-year-olds for math and science. He would be encouraged to join Dr. Garrett's Lab Rats (never mind that we'd already knew he would). For English, history, and geography, he'd be in a pod with thirteen-year-olds. He wasn't as far behind as I'd thought. He was also in his age group for phys ed, although, apparently, that pod was mostly made up of male athletes. Nick had chosen a music pod focusing on guitar for his arts pod, and the kids were of all ages in that one. There was one final pod for social consciousness, and that would include sex ed, health, and social graces, whatever that meant, and again, Nick was in his age group.

When Nick came running up to me at two-thirty, he was ecstatic.

"Mom! They're gonna let me knit in class!" He tackled me with one of his more exuberant hugs. "And I won't be the only boy knitting."

I squeezed him back, laughed. "Really? That's terrific."

"I really like this place," he told me as we walked across campus to the science building. It was on the other side of the performing arts building from humanities and next to the administration building. With eight floors, it was the tallest building on campus because it also housed the Engineering department. Randall's lab and office were on the fifth floor.

There were four other Lab Rats: Kristie, Tina, Nathan, and Monroe. Kristie was fourteen, soon to be fifteen. Tina and Nathan were both sixteen. Monroe was the oldest, at seventeen. He was blond, a little pudgy, and looked at Nick with a sigh, as if he expected to be stuck babysitting. Neither Tina nor Nathan paid much attention to Nick. They seemed more than a little absorbed in each other. Both had brown hair and were about the same average size. Tina wore glasses. If Monroe was less than thrilled about a younger kid, Kristie, who had short brown hair and a tall, slender figure, was filled with utter disdain.

"Have you guys thought about what experiments you want to do for this quarter?" Randall asked the other four.

Tina said that she and Nathan wanted to do something with peptides, I think. Monroe and Kristie each had projects that made even less sense to me. Randall had them start drafting their plans, then took Nick around the lab, explaining the equipment and the safety rules. Sid showed up around then and gave me a quick kiss. Randall gave Nick a folder full of potential projects to look through, then took Sid into the glassed-walled enclosure that was Randall's office.

I followed and hung in the doorway. "Randall, is there a health center nearby? I wrenched my back this morning and can't find my pain pills."

"Oh, yeah. It's on the outer ring of buildings between here and Performing Arts. Faculty and family have full access." Randall shut the door and sat down at the desk, which was on a raised platform so that Randall could see everything going on in the lab.

I made my way there. The health center building was huge, and I realized it also contained all the classrooms for the pre-med, nursing, and pharmacy programs on campus. The center itself was mostly empty, but then, school hadn't started yet. A student aide got my name, well, the one I was using, and found me on the computer as a faculty wife. There were still forms to fill out, as there always are.

Another student, this one from the nursing program, took me back into the exam area, which was laid out a lot like an emergency department, with a row of curtained cubicles. I could hear harsh coughing coming from one and another student nurse, leaving the cubicle, slid back the curtain far enough for me to get a glimpse of a brown-haired young man, about medium build, wearing a hospital gown that had fallen down his left arm. I started when I realized that the thin drawing on his bare shoulder was a swastika tattoo. He coughed again and pulled the gown up.

I was shown to another curtained room and was examined in no time. The x-ray took a little longer, but I was soon given a prescription for Motrin, an ice pack, and a list of instructions on how to care for my back.

The pharmacy was down the hall from the health center, and again, was relatively empty except for the kid I'd already seen, still coughing. It felt like it took forever, but it only took a few minutes, and I had my drugs and a heating pad, and was on my way back to the science building.

"You know, the first thing we'll do is find those other pills," I grumbled as Sid drove us home.

"I'm glad you bought the heating pad, though."

"Yeah, but twenty-five bucks? Not in the budget."

"We'll be fine."

At dinner, Nick waxed enthusiastic about the lab and the different projects he was debating working on.

"It's real research, too," he said. "Not just the kind of setup experiment where you know what you're supposed to get. Dr. Randall said that nobody is going to write a doctoral thesis on this stuff. They're just fun projects. Still, it's totally awesome that we're supposed to work like real scientists."

Sid and I both smiled at him, then after we cleaned up after dinner, sent him to his room to do some of his homework from his school back home.

January 8, 1987

Sid was at the university that Thursday afternoon when Mimi Dearing and Raylene Howard came by the house. I was fairly sure the two had planned it that way.

Raylene was somewhat shorter than me, though it wasn't obvious because her improbably golden hair was piled on top of her head a la Dolly Parton. Mimi had Parton's figure, and her shorter brown hair had been poufed and glued into place. Both wore dark, skin-tight, polyester pants and colorful big sweaters with huge shoulder pads. Raylene carried a steaming casserole dish in a quilted wrapping.

"We just wanted to welcome you to the neighborhood," Mimi said, once they'd introduced themselves.

"Please come in." I smiled and admitted the two women. "Would you like some tea?"

"That would be nice." Raylene smiled, then presented me with the casserole. "Oh, and here's a nice little covered dish. You can keep it warm in your oven for dinner tonight."

"That's very kind of you." I took the casserole, set it on the counter between the kitchen and the living room, and lifted the lid. "Doesn't that smell nice? Thank you very much. Why don't you ladies have a seat in the living room? I'll just pop this in the oven and get some water on."

When Sid, Nick, and I hadn't been at the university that week, we'd worked hammer and tongs at getting the boxes unpacked and the place in order. The living room was in the best shape. We'd even found some time to hang a couple of lithographs we'd had for several years that we'd replaced the summer before with nicer pieces. The furniture was basic over-stuffed, nothing terribly expensive, but in good condition. The couch was a dark navy blue dotted with huge brown and yellow flowers and the two easy chairs were brown wide-wale corduroy. A bookshelf lined the back wall of the room and overflowed with books of all kinds.

Raylene and Mimi wandered the room as I turned up the heat under the kettle on the stove and prepped the teapot. I placed the casserole in the oven on low heat, then pulled three mis-matched mugs from the cupboard, glad that we had several. Mimi looked intently at the chrome and black dinette set we'd set up in the dining area, as if she were trying to find marks on the tabletop. Three straw placemats were set at our places, each with a blue and yellow cloth napkin in a straw napkin ring. An antique kettle with a Pennsylvania Dutch motif on it sat on the fourth placemat in the middle of the table, but closer to the one end, so it was not exactly centered.

"Who plays the piano?" Raylene asked, running her fingers over the keyboard cover.

"Charles," I said. "He's a wonderful musician, but he decided he liked history better."

"My husband is chair of the history department." Raylene's smile took on an all too meaningful edge.

"How wonderful," I said. "How long have you been at the university?"

"Twenty-five years this past fall." Raylene sighed, proudly. "We'd just gotten married. I was so proud that Carl had gotten such a prestigious position so early in his career."

"Who wouldn't be?" I smiled and got out a tray from another cupboard and found a sugar bowl. "Do you ladies like milk in your tea?"

"No, thank you," said Raylene.

"Mimi?"

"No, I don't care for any, thank you."

The kettle shrieked that the water was boiling, so I rinsed the pot with some, then put in four teaspoons of the loose tea, and found the strainer. After filling the teapot with the hot water, I went through the cupboards looking for something resembling a cookie. Sid does not like sweets and is pretty firm about us eating healthy. Anticipating the need to be neighborly, I had insisted on buying a package of nice sugar cookies. I finally found them behind the tea things. I frowned. The package had been opened.

"I hope there are enough of these," I said, putting the cookies on a small plate. "I have an almost teen-age son and it is impossible to keep food in the house for any length of time."

"Isn't it, though?" Mimi giggled. "My Jimmy goes through a half gallon of milk a day, and a jar of peanut butter in three."

I brought the tray into the living room and set it on the ebony coffee table. The ladies sat down on the sofa.

"Raylene? Would you like some sugar?" I asked, pouring the first mug of tea through the strainer.

"Why, yes. Thank you."

I handed her the mug, then the sugar bowl.

I poured again. "Mimi, are you attached to the university?"

"My husband is one of the math professors," Mimi said.

"Sugar?" I asked, as I handed her the second mug I'd poured.

"Yes, thank you."

Raylene was done with the sugar bowl, so I handed it to Mimi, then poured a mug of tea for myself.

"This is so fancy with the tea," Raylene said, nonetheless picking a bit of tea leaf from her tongue.

"Charles has had to spend a fair amount of time in England for his research," I said. "That's how we picked up the tea habit."

Randall and I had selected Renaissance England as Sid/Charles' specialty largely because everyone else on the faculty specialized in American history topics or classical Greece and Rome. There was one person who taught Asian history, but I don't remember if that was her actual specialty or not. Also, thanks to my work on Shakespeare and Randall's work on Medieval and Renaissance Europe, Sid stood a better chance of pulling that one off.

"I don't think I've ever heard of the Cavendish Fellowship," Raylene said with a devious smile.

So, she'd read the Curriculum Vitae we'd assembled for Sid's alter ego. It didn't surprise me.

"It's strictly for Renaissance scholars," I said. "It's an obscure one, to be sure. But it got us to England and paid the bills, so I was grateful for it." I smiled back at Raylene. "I understand Dr. Howard is a U.S. Civil War man, writing on the Confederacy."

"Yes." Raylene blinked at the comeback. "His biography of Robert E. Lee is very highly regarded."

Irene had told me the high regard was mostly in the former Confederate states.

"Well, of course." I smiled. "I am so glad you ladies came over."

Mimi simpered. "We wanted to give you a chance to get things in some order before we did."

"How very thoughtful." I sighed. "It's been a lot of work and we did get a very unpleasant surprise the morning after we moved in. We found a whole bunch of footprints under our bedroom window. It had to have been after the snow stopped that night. We were watching so that we could be sure to get the sidewalks cleared in time."

Mimi's smile got very tight, as did Raylene's.

"That sounds frightening," Raylene said with an evil glance at Mimi.

"I know." I shrugged. "Why would anybody be spying on us?"

Raylene cleared her throat, then reached over and patted my hand. "Well, don't you worry about it, dear. It was probably just some student."

"Oh, you're right." I smiled at her, then looked right at Mimi. "I don't know why I didn't think of that."

Raylene put her finished mug down on the coffee table. "Well, I think it's time we got out of your way."

We all stood and Raylene and Mimi headed for the front door.

"Oh, Raylene," I asked. "Is the casserole dish yours? I'd like to make sure it gets back to you okay."

She pasted on another fake smile. "Yes, dear. Thank you."

"I'm sure it will be delicious. So kind of you to think of us."

"You're very sweet."

The two left quickly, to my immense relief. They were exactly the sort of women that made me cringe. Narrow-minded busybodies intent on controlling me and everyone around them. And yet... It had been kind of fun to play around with them, especially regarding those footprints under our bedroom window. I put the tea things back on the tray and brought it all back to the kitchen.

Sid came home just before four that afternoon, while I was rinsing out the teapot.

"You're home early," I said with a happy smile as Sid put his parka on the hook near the front door.

"Yeah." He sighed. "Randall's convinced I've got it down and had to referee a shouting match between the Lab Rats. Our boy said he wanted to stay and keep working. He said he could walk home. I told him to be sure and be here by five-thirty. How's your day been?"

"Well, I've almost got our bedroom done, and the den looks pretty much taken care of, although there are still several boxes in there. I've got water in the kettle."

Sid slid up behind me, pulling me close against him, and letting his hands wander.

"Okay," I said, enjoying the feeling. "What time is our son likely to be home?"

Sid nuzzled my ear. "If he's out of that lab before five, it will be a miracle." Okay, he may have added a certain curse word before miracle. "And I don't believe in miracles."

I do, and he knew it. But Sid's a confirmed atheist and I'm strongly religious and Catholic, specifically. We were still trying to figure out what to do about the church thing.

"Okay." I laughed. "Maybe a fast one."

Sid was already halfway undressed.

Fortunately, when Nick finally got home, Sid was in the bathroom, finishing his second shave of the day, something he sorely needed to do if it would not become obvious he'd changed his hair color. Nick still realized what his dad and I had been up to. I know because he took one look at me and rolled his eyes. The poor kid had been going to sleep with his headphones on as it was.

The reality is when your sex life is as exuberant as mine and Sid's is, well, you're going to get caught every now and then. Nick was, like most kids, grossed out by the idea of his parents having S-E-X, but only partly grossed out. Sid had been raised believing in free love and that sex was simply normal, natural behavior. So, that made it a lot easier for us to talk to Nick about sex, and he'd admitted that as grossed out as he was, it was still pretty cool that his parents loved each other that much. He also scored lots of points on the long-suffering front for having to deal with such noisy parents.

"When's dinner?" Nick asked as Sid came in from the bathroom.

"As soon as I make it," Sid replied with genial annoyance.

"Maybe not," I said.

I explained about the visit and the casserole and pulled it out of the oven. I know I told Raylene and Mimi that it smelled good. I'd lied. The smell was marginal, at best. Nick grimaced and shook his head when I pulled it out of the oven. Sid was brave enough to take a taste.

He spat it out. "Someone just cooked some ground beef in some canned mushroom soup and added ketchup."

I got a spoon and took a taste, too. "Oh, my god. You're right."

"My aunt would have done better." Sid shook his head.

Sid's aunt, Stella, raised him after Sid's mother had been killed when Sid was two. He used to joke that his aunt had never wanted him and proved it by trying to kill him with her cooking. As it turned out, Stella had wanted him very badly. She was just a terrible, terrible cook.

"She would have burned it," Nick said. He took a taste and gagged. "I can't eat that."

Given that anything remotely edible within Nick's grasp was sucked up at the speed of light, that was saying something.

I winced. "I hate wasting food."

"You didn't waste it, darling," Sid said. "Whoever made that atrocity did."

"We'll have to find a way to be nice about it." I sighed. "She offered it as a gift. That's the Christian thing to do."

"I'm not a Christian," Sid said firmly.

"Yes. But she's married to your boss, and she seems to like playing that card."

Sid rolled his eyes. "Let's see. What's on the menu for tonight?"

Sid and I had planned out our meals for the week after we'd gotten groceries that Monday night.

"Chicken," said Nick, grinning mischievously.

I chuckled as Sid shook his head. Given that Sid rarely eats red meat, we eat a lot of chicken. We'd found some frozen fish fillets that hadn't been breaded, but we'd finished those the night before. Sid tussled briefly with Nick, then checked the list stuck to the refrigerator door with a magnet from Stonehenge.

"Well, aren't you lucky, smart-ass." Sid opened the pantry door and got out tomato sauce, a jar of artichokes in oil, some pasta, and a can of black olives. "We're having spaghetti with artichoke sauce."

We were eating a lot of pasta. My heavy appetite was bad enough, but with Nick's still on full overdrive, there were plenty of chinks to fill and we were on a budget.

"Why don't you help your mother make a salad?" Sid told Nick as he got out a small saucepan.

It was tight in that kitchen, but as much as I hate cooking, it wasn't so bad working alongside Nick and Sid. Since we were supposedly moving an established household, we'd decided that it was reasonable for us to have a lot of the dried herbs and spices that we had at home, and that helped a lot, since there was not nearly as much of a variety in the supermarket as we were used to.

We chatted about our respective days. Mine had been spent trying to finish the unpacking. Sid had set up his office at the university and spent the day reading. Nick's day had more variety, but he was mostly taken with his English lesson.

"We're supposed to be studying a Shakespeare play this quarter," Nick told us as we ate. "Only the theatre department at the university is doing Richard the Third, so the teachers decided we're going to read that one. And for history we're going to be doing a unit on the Wars of the Roses because that's what the play's about."

"Well, the end of it, yes," I said. "And keep in mind, the play is basically Elizabethan propaganda. Some of the events may have some relation to what really happened, but the guy that wrote the play was working for the granddaughter of the guy that killed Richard."

Nick looked over at his father. "Dad, did you know that?"

"Actually, I did."

The phone rang and Sid got up and answered it.

Nick continued. "Oh, and get this. The guy directing the play? He came in and asked if any of us wanted to audition for the young princes. I think I might, Mom. That could be really fun."

"I found out the other day that I'll have to audition, too, so why not?" I smiled at him.

Sid had just returned to the table with a sigh. "Looks like this Richard the Third thing may end up a family party. That was Carl Howard. He wants me to work with the Test School on teaching the Wars of the Roses. I have to come up with several enrichment lectures over the course of the quarter." He looked at me. "I'll need your help with that."

"And we get to audition for the play, Dad."

Sid looked at me, his eyebrow lifted.

"Honey, the odds are against either Nick or I getting parts."

Sid shook his head. "I'm willing to bet Nick knows Shakespeare better than his peers, and you certainly do." He sighed. "And we all have to be pretty good actors at times."

The three of us looked at each other, feeling the tension. Our covers were as close to our real lives as possible. But, yeah, we were essentially playing characters and if we weren't believable, the result could be deadly.

AMATEUR THEATRICALS

After kitchen clean up, Nick was sent to his room to finish his Test School homework and to put some time in on his homework from back home.

"Honey, you have to get it done," I told Nick as he sighed loudly. "I know it's a lot of work, but the school at home thinks we're teaching you while we're doing our ghost-writing thing."

The ghost writing was what we told our families and friends back home to explain why the three of us were away for an extended period of time. It was a terrific excuse because we were "contractually obligated" not to tell anyone what specifically we were doing, let alone for whom.

Nick winced. "It's just boring, Mom." He sighed. "Is high school going to be as boring?"

"I hope not."

We had gotten Nick signed up at a boy's Catholic high school that had a solid reputation for challenged their students. My nephew Darby, who was one of Nick's best friends, and Nick's other best friend, Josh Sandoval, would be going there, too. But that was almost six months away, and there were no guarantees that Nick wouldn't be bored there, too. In fact, I was worried that he'd be so far ahead of his classmates, he wouldn't fit in when we got home. But there was nothing to be done about it. At least he was having fun in the meantime.

I found Sid in the den, where there were about five more boxes to unpack. The room was crammed with a small wooden desk, a loveseat, a couple bookshelves, and a small television set, sitting on top of a VCR. The TV had an antenna on the top, as well. We didn't think there'd be a lot of time to watch it, so we decided against buying cable TV.

"The room looks good," Sid said, opening one of the boxes. He frowned at the contents. "Where did you get all these books?"

"I went a lot of places."

Sid shook his head. "Well, nobody is going to question us based on not having enough books." He looked up at me. "How's your back doing?"

"Still pretty stiff, but I'm mostly mobile."

"You shouldn't have spent these past two days unpacking."

I rolled my eyes. "Resting it doesn't help. And I worked out on the weight machines today. Between that and the walk there and back, I'm feeling better." I sat on the arm of the loveseat, which was covered in gray, speckled Herculon. "So, besides working with Randall and reading, have you looked over those police reports?"

"Finally." Sid shuddered.

The four dead agents were Rod Stinsky, Damian Walsh, Maria Agnotti, and Troy Hill, with Stinsky being the one who'd died right before Christmas. Agnotti, Hill, and Stinsky had been science and engineering majors. Walsh had been studying languages. Each of the victims had been strangled by hand. The first three had been hit over the head from behind before they died. Stinsky had been shoved face-first into the snow, then strangled. The bodies had been found all over campus and had been moved after death. Snowfall after Stinsky had been dumped had obliterated any tracks.

The police had been trying to find some link between them and hadn't found anything. Walsh and Hill had had a couple math classes together, but that was it. As far as the police could tell, none of them knew each other. As I thought about it, we had no way of knowing whether they and the other KGB students knew each other.

"Strangled by hand, though," I said. "That's the weird thing. I mean, these people were presumably trained in hand-to-hand combat and in evasionary tactics. It almost seems like they were attacked by someone they knew and trusted."

"It depends on how they got hit on the head." Sid shrugged. "As much as I don't like the thought, the reality is someone could get the drop on us and knock us dopey enough not to fight back."

"I like to think it would take somebody darned good."

Sid chuckled. "It would. But it also gives us something to look for."

"True." I suddenly frowned. "Oh. I was going to tell you earlier, before you got me all distracted. I think Mimi Dearing may, in fact, be our nosy next-door neighbor. I asked her and Raylene about the footprints under the window the other day and Raylene kept glaring at her."

Sid's eyebrow lifted. "Dearing..."

"He's a math professor."

"Well, we stand warned." He looked up at me and grinned. "Would you like to engage in a continuation of this afternoon's activity?"

I smiled. "I was just about to ask you the same thing."

January 9 – 11, 1987

I almost felt as though I was going on stage that next evening. There are two things that scare me. One is corpses. I'd been getting better about those, but they still freak me out when I run across them. The other is parties where I don't know anyone. That night there was the big all-faculty dinner at the Socratic Society Center.

The Socratic was more like a fancy club than anything else, reserved solely for the use of faculty members, although faculty members could bring in a guest or two. Family members were considered guests. The center was on the third floor of the Commons building and once the elevator opened, there was a guard at the desk to make sure anyone going in was a member of the faculty or was with a member of the faculty.

Sid and I checked our parkas at the coat check next to the guard desk. Under his, Sid had put on a sport coat over a mostly blue Fair Isles sweater I'd made him that fall with a dress shirt and tie underneath. I had on a dark gray cashmere dress. I'd bought it two or three years before because it was so simple and gorgeous, with slightly padded shoulders, a turtleneck, narrow long sleeves, fitted waist, and full A-line skirt that hit just below my knees. Because Sid and I live in L.A., I almost never wore it because it seldom got cool enough to be comfortable in cashmere. In wintry Kansas, I figured I could, and the dress was old enough to call it a hand-me-down or thrift shop special, thus making it consistent with our cover. I had on black, knee-high boots with a short, spiked heel, as well. A narrow black patent leather belt, a modest pearl necklace and earrings completed the ensemble. The one problem with the dress is that it hugged my body, and my bra showed as a result, so I'd ditched the bra.

The Socratic consisted of a dining room, with sparkling white linen tablecloths on round tables and leather wingback chairs, a club room, with more overstuffed leather chairs, and a lounge, which was essentially an elegantly appointed bar. Sid had told me that lunch and dinner were both available and while the prices were reasonable, I was still worried about the budget.

We did not have to pay for dinner that night, although we were only given one drink ticket apiece. I opted for a glass of white wine, and it was a rather good one. Irene arrived shortly after Sid and I did, and the two of us women settled into a pair of chairs in the clubroom. Sid got commandeered by Carl Howard, a portly man in a gray suit, glasses, and thinning hair on top that he tried to disguise by combing the remaining hair over the bald spot.

"Where's Randall?" I asked Irene.

She laughed as she sipped her Seven and Seven. "Oh, he never goes to these things."

"That's right." I smiled.

"He's been telling me some nice things about your boy."

"Ryan's having the time of his life." I couldn't help laughing. "He gave me an extended discourse this afternoon on why sloppy lab technique is such a bad thing, which I hope means fewer messes at home."

"I wish I could say it will." Irene giggled a little.

"Oh, dear." I glanced around, then lowered my voice. "Is it my imagination, or are at least a third of the guys in this room packing heat?"

Irene laughed loudly. "You mean the guns? They're not supposed to, especially around students, but, yeah, they carry, and no one tells them not to. Kind of how it works in this area."

"That's a little scary." I sighed. "What can you tell me about Mimi Dearing and Raylene Howard?"

"Well, you know Raylene is the ringleader of the Faculty Wives." Irene rolled her eyes. "Isabel Lovegood technically outranks her, but I think Isabel just loves fomenting trouble while keeping her hands clean. Mimi is a lesser member."

"I got that bit of hierarchy. They came by the house yesterday. The interesting thing is, Raylene bragged about her husband. Mimi didn't. She just said he was a math professor."

"Clarence Dearing is only one of the top mathematicians in the country, possibly the world." Irene shook her head. "Trust me, nobody cares about Raylene's husband except a few Southerners who are still lamenting the War of Northern Aggression."

I frowned. "So, if Mimi's husband is technically more distinguished..."

"It doesn't mean a thing. For one thing, Raylene has Isabel's blessing. For another, Mimi hates her husband's guts." Irene sighed. "It's the whole sad dynamic of that group. I couldn't elaborate on Sunday for a lot of reasons.

There are probably fifteen, sixteen wives who consider themselves part of the club. Almost all of their husbands are tenured faculty. Most of the associates' wives also must work to make a living. Seven of Raylene's crew are the inner circle, including Mimi, by the way. All of them are very traditional housewives. The problem is, they're also incredibly intelligent. They'd have to be to attract their husbands. Which means they're bored out of their minds. But they want to be good wives, so instead of doing things like taking classes or finding jobs they like, they make trouble for everyone else. Frankly, if I were more of a sociologist, I think it would make a fascinating case study."

I shrugged. "Or you could look at how the social messages they received affected them."

Irene's gaze slid over to Raylene Howard, who had just draped herself over her husband's arm. I looked around for Sid but didn't see him.

"That's an idea." Irene laughed softly. "I think I even have a decent sample size to work with, too, not to mention a couple nice control groups in the working wives and the ones who do not participate." She looked at me. "I've been doing some really fun work on gender messaging in our society. The Faculty Wives would make a good case study." She sighed suddenly. "The problem is, they have some significant influence on their husbands who also have significant control over tenure."

"That's not getting any better, is it?" I grimaced. It had been a major problem in Wisconsin.

"We've only been here two years. And my department chair is perfectly happy." Irene blinked quickly. "And if I'm honest, Randall and I aren't entirely sure we want to stay here. It's the whole Company thing, although I think

Randall is a little unduly optimistic that we'll eventually be able to outrun it. The problem is that neither of us are spring chickens. We need to settle somewhere. We just don't know where yet."

A gong sounded and Irene and I got up as everyone else started toward the dining room. Sid waved at us from a table in the back corner of the room, and Irene and I went over. The one blessing was that our table was almost filled by that point with several faculty women and Drs. Jeff and Serena Necht. Serena also taught in the theatre department, but I don't remember what. Jeff taught theatre history, and I had one of his sections. They were across the table from us, so I really didn't get a chance to talk to them.

I also discovered about then that I had made a serious tactical error in wearing the cashmere dress.

"Well, well, well," said Beverly Mott, who had landed on Irene's other side from me. "Looks like you've made yourself an enemy."

My jaw dropped. "I have?"

Grinning, Bev glanced over at Raylene, and I realized she'd been shooting daggers at me all evening.

"But I was very nice to her," I said, trying not to whimper.

Bev laughed. She was a tall woman with a full figure and draped in colorful fabrics. She taught costuming, and I realized I had one of her classes, too.

"That only rubs salt in the wound." Bev cackled. She gave me the once over. "My darling, every straight man in this room and we lesbians have been drooling since you walked in. My god, have you no idea how sexy you look tonight?"

Sid sighed loudly. "Trust me, she doesn't."

"But I'm not." I glared at him.

[Oh, but you were and are. I spent that entire evening cursing the assholes making crude jokes about how much they wanted to jump your bones and debating whether I wanted to take some time to enjoy the feel of your luscious curves under that lovely soft wool or just jump you as fast as I could. - SEH]

We got through dinner pleasantly enough, but then I noticed not only was Raylene shooting daggers at me, so were Mimi and several other women, as well. After dinner, Sid and I were chatting with Bob and Cheryl Westin. Bob was also in the history department, and Cheryl was a nurse at the local hospital. Raylene pasted on a fake smile and slid up to us.

"Charles, Linda, I'm so glad to see you getting to know the rest of our department." She took my arm and gently pulled. "Linda, darling, may I speak to you privately for a second?"

"Sure, Raylene." I nodded at Bob and Cheryl, then followed Raylene to what I guessed was not an entirely private corner.

Raylene smiled again. "Linda, darling, please understand I have your best interests at heart, and I know there is no way you could possibly know all the ins and outs of how things operate here at Collins. So, let me help you. I would not, for the world, want you to think I believe it, but there is a nasty little rumor floating around that you and your husband got noisy enough in your bedroom earlier this week that the police were alerted."

"Oh." I smiled my best fake smile, too. "It's probably what those footsteps under our window were about. I told you about that yesterday, didn't I?"

"Yes, you did."

"Somebody was spying on us. Although it is true that my husband is quite the man, shall we say?"

"Oh." Raylene coughed lightly in consternation. "What about your poor son? It must be terribly embarrassing for him."

"We make sure he's asleep. That's why the footsteps were so frightening. They had obviously been made after ten o'clock that night because that's when the snow stopped. Why would somebody want to stand outside our window on a snowy night? And now there's that rumor?"

I shook my head. "Raylene, I don't want to think there's a connection to someone on the faculty. I hope you can help me find out who's behind this."

She simpered. "Of course. Thank you for having this little chat with me."

She slunk away. I sighed. I most certainly had an enemy there.

Sid, for his part, seemed bent on giving the rumor a boost. I felt his hand on my backside several times as we said good night to various other couples. Later, as he helped me on with my coat, his hand just happened to rub against my breasts. Nick was asleep when we got home and, fortunately, had put on his headphones. Sid didn't wait to undress me or take me to the bedroom. [Oh, yeah. The best of both worlds. God, I loved that dress. - SEH]

Saturday, we stayed in until noon or so, lounging a little, then doing chores. A snowstorm had started the night before and didn't really stop until eleven that morning. The three of us played in the snow, then Sid and Nick got the shoveling done. After that, it was off to the grocery store and to make a couple phone calls.

One of the challenges of working a job like we were on was that we had family back home that expected to hear from us periodically. When Sid and I had worked that case in Wisconsin, we'd each made a point of getting away once a week and calling those we needed to from a pay phone using special calling cards that would make it hard to trace where the call was coming from. We'd decided to do the same thing this time around.

I called my sister Mae first. The kids were back in school, and she had some news.

"I got into the MLS program," she said.

"At SC?" I meant the University of Southern California.

"Of course." Mae chuckled.

Mae's husband Neil teaches at the dental school there, which helped on the fee side. She had been talking about going for her Master of Library Science for the past year, but had put off applying because her youngest child, Lissy, was only six months old.

"That's terrific, Mae. I'm really happy for you."

Mae caught the catch in my voice, though. "You don't sound all that happy."

"It's not that." I swallowed. "I just don't want you getting mad at me."

"Why would getting into library school get me mad at you?"

"Uh, my husband talked me into applying for PhD programs last fall." I made a face. "I didn't know you were applying for your master's. Really, I didn't."

"Oh." Mae's pause was tense, at best. "Okay. You didn't know because I didn't tell you, so obviously you weren't trying to outdo me."

"I'm really not."

"Then how do you keep doing it, anyway?"

"I haven't been accepted anywhere yet. And it's been several years since my master's, so I may not get in."

Mae laughed, the bitterness in her voice fading. "It's okay, Lisa. I can get my doctorate, too, eventually."

"And you're doing this raising six kids and working part time. That's way more than I have to deal with."

"So's how your out-of-town job going?"

"We're settling in. Have you heard from Mama and Daddy?"

She had, and the news was the normal. I finally had to put her off so the Sid could call his aunt, Stella, and Sy Flournoy, her lover. Nick talked to Stella, too. He was, for all intents and purposes, her grandson, and she adored the boy.

Sid made one other phone call. We had one other member of our team who would not be on the campus but would come by periodically to say hello and bring mail from home for us and the rest of our team members. I was a little puzzled by Sid's request. We hadn't brought any photos of us from home because of the whole need to change how we look. Plus, we didn't want to bring anything that we'd regret losing just in case somebody tried to take us out by blowing up our place.

Once Sid hung up, though, he looked at me and smiled pensively.

"What?" I asked.

"You called me your husband," he said.

Okay, the whole being married thing had been tough for me to get used to, which was why I'd been referring to Sid as my spouse rather than my husband.

I shrugged. "I've had to refer to you that way a few times this week. I guess I'm getting used to it."

"Okay." Sid looked at me again and nodded. "We've got groceries to get."

We went to church that Sunday. Oddly enough, it was Sid's idea. Sid's an atheist and always has been. However, Carl Howard had strongly hinted that he expected the people in his department to go to church, so Sid had found the local Catholic church and the mass times, and we went. Nick was not enthused. Truth be told, neither was I. The sermon was pedantic, the choir barely adequate, and no one on the altar was female, unlike our parish at home.

"Details," Sid reminded me as we drove home.

"How is Carl Howard going to know whether or not we're going to church?"

"Two of the other department members were in the pews."

I sighed. At least, we'd set ourselves up as a mixed marriage. Sid had been around me long enough he could almost pull off appearing as Catholic, but there were a lot of little things that I did that I didn't even think about which Sid would find awkward and would only make it obvious he wasn't Catholic. We didn't need that.

"Honey," Sid continued. "I know we don't technically care about sticking around here, but we need to look as though we do."

"Believe me, darling, I understand." I sighed. "Been there, done that, especially on the academic side. The question is, how desperate do you want to be?"

"That's a tough one. I am a family man."

"And I have a career to back you up." Part of our cover story was that I'd taught high school English while he'd gotten his degrees. I sighed. "Funny thing is, honey, one of the things I learned in Wisconsin is that sometimes acting like you don't care gets you more than if you freak out and totally cave into the expectations."

"You guys keep talking about Wisconsin," Nick said from the back seat. "Is that how you know Dr. Randall and Dr. Irene?"

Sid and I both looked back at him. Sid rolled his eyes, and I smiled.

"Yes," I said. "Remember when we had that ghost writing project the fall of nineteen-eighty-four and were gone for so long?"

Nick's jaw dropped. "You weren't ghost writing. And, Mom, you came back way after Dad did."

"I was the one teaching, and I had to finish the quarter," I said. "However, we really can't say more than that. Do you understand?"

Nick winced. "I guess not. That sucks, though."

"It does," said Sid. "But it's how it goes, as you well know. At least you're with us on this one."

"Yeah." Nick grinned.

The poor thing. He had no idea.

To Breanna, 6/24/00
Today's Topic: More About the Side Business
Yesterday we were dealing with the heavier aspects of my parents' side business and how it affected all of us. It's still hard for me to talk about it. The whole secrecy thing is such a reflex. I know that seems a little dysfunctional, but for us, it literally was about staying alive. It also made the three of us really close. That's why I talk to them every day. I

like talking to them. In some ways, they're as much my best friends as you and Darby and Josh are.

I remember sometime after they got put on overt status that I tried to tell a girl about their business. She was horrified that my parents made me keep their secret. Yeah, it was tough on me, but it was either keep the secret or not have them. Having them was a lot better than not, believe me.

I guess, too, that I'm still trying to get over that they told you about the side business. I don't know if Mom's just trying to get more open about it or what, but it was a total surprise. And that story Dad told about how one of their agents blew his cover during a case they were on in Wisconsin. I'd never heard that story before. I knew they'd worked a case in Wisconsin, back in '84, before Dad gave up sleeping around. That was the first time I've ever heard Dad tell a story about their work that way.

It was fun, though, and I think it really helped his mood. That's why I could tell you about the Kansas case last night.

We spent the afternoon talking about the play and the real history of Richard the Third. Nick helped Sid make dinner while I worked on my monologue for the upcoming audition.

I'd like to say that Sid and I got a good, solid night's sleep that Sunday night. Or that we'd been up to something so entertaining, we, um, didn't get to sleep right away. Alas, neither was the case. Sid was nervous about the next day, and I couldn't really blame him.

The thing is, Sid is a darned good teacher. He'd been teaching my nephew Darby how to play piano for several years at that point and was starting to help at Stella's music school. He'd even given a short talk at my church's youth camp the previous summer.

But while he likes history, he is not a historian, at least, not in the academic sense. So, I could understand that he was feeling pretty nervous about his first day of teaching Western Civilization. He had two sections coming up that Monday morning, and kept going over his notes for his lecture, when he wasn't prowling the house, mumbling to himself.

That night, it took forever for him to get to sleep. Sid talks in his sleep a lot. I've gotten to the point that if I don't hear him, I can't sleep. By the time the nightly monologue started, I was exhausted. Then Sid had a nightmare. He'd served in Vietnam, visibly as an army corporal and actually as an intelligence agent. When he's tense or upset, he dreams about the first time he'd killed someone, which that night, of course, woke me up. I didn't mind being soothing - he'd done the same for me countless times. But that meant neither of us got that much sleep.

January 12 – 13, 1987

Monday morning, I did not want to get up. Fortunately, there hadn't been any snow that night, which meant no shoveling before heading out. That didn't stop Sid from nudging me out of bed around six. Nick had to be at school by eight. Sid wanted to hit the treadmills at the fitness center in plenty of time to change for his first class at nine. Which meant all three of us were out the door by six-thirty.

At seven a.m., we all were on adjacent treadmills. The machines had been set up so that you could watch one of the TVs mounted in a row above the huge glass window overlooking an icy walkway to the rest of the campus. After half an hour, Nick left to get dressed for school. He also had his physical education pod later that day. He popped up just before we were done. Sid and I stopped running long enough for Nick to kiss us goodbye, and he headed off. We finished our hour-long run. Sid kissed me, then headed for the showers. I went to the weight room and did my workout to protect my back.

Sid met me at the door to the locker rooms, dressed in a sport coat, slacks, and snowy-white dress shirt.

"Hey, I'm off," he said, his demeanor so cool I knew he was totally freaking out.

I grabbed his face and gave him a solid kiss. "You are going to knock them dead. I've seen you teach before. You're good at this."

"I'm glad you think so, lover." He smiled and handed me a key. "Not that you need it, but it will look better if you have a key to my office. Go ahead and leave your stuff there."

"Thanks. I love you."

"I love you, too."

I went into the locker room and got showered and dressed in jeans, Oxford shirt, and sweater, then put my workout clothes in my gym bag. The running shoes I wore. You would think I'd be wearing snow boots, but these were special running shoes, with a false bottom that I could pop open and pull out a stiletto, a screwdriver, batteries for a transmitter, another transmitter, and things like that. Those shoes had saved my backside more than once.

Sid was just leaving his office when I arrived there right before nine. It was on the second floor, not far from the bridge to the performing arts building. I gave him another kiss and quick pep talk, then he left. The office was small, just room enough for the desk and chair, a chair in front of the desk, a couple file cabinets and a small bookshelf on the wall. On the other hand, it wasn't shared, so that was something. I set the gym bag on the side of the desk furthest from the door, then hoisted my daypack on my shoulder and got myself out of there.

My first class that day was at ten a.m. It was Voice and Diction with Dr. Dorfmann, who reminded us that not only were we required to audition for both Top Girls and Richard III that Wednesday and Thursday, he did not want to hear any monologues from Richard III. I swallowed. I'd found one from Hamlet that I thought would work, but was struggling a bit with remembering all of it.

My memory is pretty darned good. It must be. But the past few years, it has been about memorizing codes and strings of numbers, addresses, and a variety of other things. I hadn't memorized lines from a play since high school.

We introduced ourselves to the class, with me explaining that I already had a bachelor's degree in another field and was taking undergrad prerequisites to eventually get my masters. I did not mention Nick or Sid and Dorfmann, bless him, didn't say anything, either.

There was an hour break between Voice and Diction and Costuming at noon. I had three sandwiches with me, plus some cut-up celery and carrots. What I wanted was potato chips and there were several vending machines next to the bridge to the Humanities building. I sighed but decided to save my change for when I'd really need the snack. I went to the room I'd seen across from the costume shop.

"Who are you?" demanded an almost stout woman with full blond hair from a chair at the table.

"Linda. I'm new." I swallowed. "You are?"

"Tracy Schultz." She was probably in her early twenties, but had a hard edge to her.

"Welcome to the Green Room," said a young man. He had a couple rolls around his middle, and a round face, brown hair that was on the edge of red, and a fully pleasant demeanor. "I'm Mark."

"Nice to meet you," I said.

I looked at the green walls and suddenly realized where I was. It was an official green room, i.e., a backstage lounge where actors can wait and rest before the play starts and between scenes. The rooms are painted green because that color is supposed to be soothing. I thought the color in this green room was somewhat more bilious than soothing, but I wasn't going to say anything. I sat down in one of the plastic chairs near the table.

"I'm guessing it's okay to eat lunch here," I said.

"If you dare," said Tracy. "This place, like, needs serious fumigating."

I pulled a sandwich from my daypack. "I've seen worse. I think."

That got a small laugh.

Costuming was at noon. Bev Mott, bless her, did not reveal my connection to the rest of the university faculty, although she winked at me as she walked into the classroom. The bad news was that I had to sign up to work at least one of the shows that would happen that quarter, plus several more hours in the costume shop. I signed up to work the Dance Recital, in the hopes of getting my hours out of the way sooner rather than later. After all, that first week or so, I was supposed to be concentrating on establishing my cover rather than investigating. After that, who knew how much time I'd have for school?

There would also be reading and exams, but the real surprise was the kid I'd seen in the Health Center the week before. He was in the class and answered to the name Terrence Peterson, and it seemed like Bev already knew him.

At two, I had Theatre history with Dr. Necht. I honestly do not believe he recognized me from the Faculty Dinner. [He had his eyes glued to your breasts that night, so I'm not surprised. - SEH] He was an amiable fellow with brown, thinning hair, a slender figure, and wire-rimmed glasses. That class was mostly about reading and a couple exams, although there was a ten-page term paper due at the end of the quarter.

"Well, that should do it for today," Dr. Necht said as he wrapped up his lecture. "Questions? Hopes, dreams, aspirations?"

I suspected there were plenty of the latter three, but no one volunteered.

From there, I hurried back to Humanities and Sid's office. Sid sat at his desk, glaring at some journal article on top.

"Well?" I asked. Okay, demanded when I got there.

He shrugged. "It went fine. No one seems fated to become a history major, which is kind of nice. The students seem like decent kids, mostly interested in filling out their general education requirements."

"That's what I figured." I smiled at him.

"So, you were right. Again." He grinned at me. "Do we let Nick walk home or hang around here long enough to drive him home?"

I couldn't help grinning. "Walking is good for his character and not being in the house lets us carry on without worrying about the noise."

Sid laughed. "That poor kid, having to walk home so often."

Both our Tuesday, Thursday classes started later than our Monday, Wednesday, Friday classes. Sid started with Research Techniques and Resources at ten in the morning, and I had acting, starting at eleven. The research class was the one Sid was really sweating, which I didn't understand. Admittedly, back home, I'm the one who does most of the paper research for our freelance writing business.

Thanks to my master's degree, I'm good at it. But Sid was mostly through his own master's program in music education by that point, so it wasn't as though he did not know how to do research. In fact, he'd gotten darned good at it. [However, I was painfully aware that I did not have the PhD I claimed and was worried that it would show. - SEH]

A light snow had fallen the night before. We sent Nick off to school by seven-thirty, then Sid and I did the shoveling work out. Sid was a little worried about my back, but I was fine. We were done well before eight-thirty. Sid showered, ate, and was out the door by nine-fifteen. I cleaned up the kitchen, took my time in the shower, then walked to class, given that I hadn't had a chance to run, and it didn't look like I was going to get one.

Professor Maggie Leitner wanted us to just call her Maggie. She not only had her MFA, she'd spent a lot of years acting in New York, both on and off Broadway. She had a deep, slightly scratchy voice and the miasma of cigarette smoke wafted off her, even though she didn't smoke in the building. Actually, no one was allowed to, except in the faculty offices.

Acting was straightforward. We each introduced ourselves, did a couple exercises, talked about motivation and intention and stuff like that. Maggie also told us that we would have to audition for both Top Girls and Richard III, then gave us a bunch of reading to do.

As soon as acting let out, I hurried over the bridge to Sid's office in the humanities building. He was there with one of his Research students, LeShawn Pile.

We knew LeShawn as our good friend Jesse White. He's a little taller than average and his skin is the color of cocoa out of the box, although he'd grown a goatee and mustache for this job. Sid made the "introductions" in the doorway, then pulled us both inside and shut the door. We all checked our bug finders almost automatically.

"How safe is it to talk in here?" LeShawn/Jesse asked.

"It's pretty soundproof," Sid said. "Ryan and I tested it out last week. I could barely hear him yelling, and I was in the office next door."

"Really?" I couldn't help grinning.

LeShawn groaned. "Come on, you two."

He got really embarrassed when Sid and I started teasing each other.

"So, what do you have?" Sid asked him.

"Not much yet. I got the pickup from Red Light this morning, but it's just the photos."

"Yeah." Sid sighed. "We need copies made and touched up to match how we look now. You can mail the prints back home when you're done. Can you do all that?"

"Oh, yeah. I brought my dark room and other stuff." Jesse shrugged. "I've got to produce some winter shots for my big show, anyway."

Jesse/LeShawn's excuse for being away was that he and his wife were going to do a photo tour of the U.S. before his wife got too far along in her pregnancy. Well, that's what they'd told their families. Kathy Deiner, who would be known to us as Karen Crombie, had discovered that she was pregnant early that December. Sid and I had offered to let the two of them sit this one out, but Kathy and Jesse both said no. Too much work had already been done and Kathy had pointed out that she'd have a tougher time doing something like this once the baby got here. Besides, she could work in financial aid and snoop discreetly, not to mention that being pregnant would make her look a lot less suspicious.

"How's Karen doing?" I asked. We'd been using our cover names instead of our own, for obvious reasons.

"Oh, she's fine." Jesse rolled his eyes. "I'm the nervous wreck, and it isn't just this job. It's the whole idea of being a father."

"Tell me about it," said Sid with a laugh. He'd resisted fairly hard when Nick's mother brought him to our doorstep. "But once I got used to the idea, it turned out to be pretty nice."

"Yeah, well, at least, I asked for it." Jesse grinned. "One of the main reasons the two of us got married was to have babies. You got anything else for me?"

"No. Thanks, though."

"I'd better get going then." He checked his watch. "I've got editing class in half an hour and homework tonight."

He glared merrily at Sid.

"It's about the practice," Sid replied.

Jesse left.

"So, what's up with the photos?" I asked. "You just said that you needed them after all the other day."

Sid rolled his eyes. "My male colleagues. Carl Howard visited me on Thursday and was surprised I didn't have any photos out. He said that family photos on the desk were the mark of a happily married man. I told him I wasn't sure where mine were, thanks to the move. I wasn't going to put any out. Then we had Friday night."

"What happened?"

"Your cashmere dress, which, by the way, I still really love." Sid winced. "I think I'm finally getting what you put up with from men. A lot of the guys that night didn't see us come in together, so they didn't realize that you were my wife. They referred to you in the coarsest possible terms and laughed about what all they could get you to do. The guys in the singles scene weren't that crude. Worse yet, when these guys weren't making jokes about you, they were running their wives down." Sid shuddered. "Anyway, I suddenly thought that maybe Carl had a point about the desk photos. And a couple for the house, just in case. Jesse's going to retouch them so that they match our cover and how we look."

"Oh. I'm sorry about that."

"Don't be." Sid got up from his desk and pulled me close to him. "My darling, you are and remain a wonderfully sexy, sensual woman, and I love that about you. But you are so much more than that. I just can't believe there are so many assholes out there who only see a plaything and not the incredibly special whole woman I know and love."

I smiled. "Do we want to talk about primary socialization and society's gender messages?"

"Later, preferably with our son, so that he keeps his head on straight." Sid suddenly grinned. "We both have a class at two, don't we?"

"Yes. And I want to eat lunch before then." I tried to look severe. "Besides, I have no interest in being your plaything."

"I have no interest in having you as a plaything." Sid nuzzled my ear, then rubbed his thumb along the back of my neck.

That one always gets me. I hissed with the pleasure.

"But I would not mind a happy, passionate celebration of our love for each other," Sid whispered.

I thanked God the office door did not have a window.

In real life, such as it is, Sid, Nick, and I live in Beverly Hills. The reason we do is that is where Sid found the first place that seemed livable when he was transferred to the L.A. area as part of Operation Quickline. This happened in 1976.

What makes this relevant is that Sid and I do know people who work in the "Industry," aka the motion picture and TV industry. It would be hard not to, given where we live. After defense industries, it is the biggest employer in the Los Angeles area. Not to mention that a lot of the bigger players live in our immediate area and somewhat to the east in West Hollywood.

So, we know what "Industry" attitude looks like. It's this weird sense of being more important than anybody else, but not quite. In fact, it's a little hard to describe, but easy to spot. Big shots who run multi-million-dollar studios have it, right along with wannabes who couldn't get arrested in town. Not everyone in the industry has the attitude. Just the assholes. But there are a lot of assholes in that business.

I arrived at the classroom for Beginning Directing about fifteen minutes early, having cleaned up and eaten. My notebook sat on the chair desk combo with a pen next to it, ready to take notes. I also sat in the front row. With my last name being Wycherly, I was alphabetized into the back of the room for almost all my education. I love the front row.

Because this was an undergraduate class, like all my others, the students were young, in their late teens, early twenties. There were a couple of serious young men. The kid named Mark that I'd met the day before was in the class. Along with five guys and eleven girls, including the perpetually grumpy Tracy Schultz, Mark wasn't terribly interested in directing, per se, but needed the credits. Two young and cute college girls sat up front near me.

As the minute hand on the classroom clock ticked past the one, the door opened, and another serious young man hurried in and took a seat in the desk on the other side from the young and cute college girls. We waited some more, the room still except for some giggling. Fifteen minutes after the class was due to start, I began to think about taking off and had gotten as far as putting my pen back into its pocket on my daypack when the door opened, and Earnest Kaspar finally made his entrance.

He was a short man with black hair, graying slightly at the temples, and wore a rust suede jacket over a blue chambray shirt and off-white chinos with white running shoes. He had no papers or notes with him, which I thought was a little odd, but decided not to question it. I wasn't really there to learn how to direct a play. I was there to protect him from whatever monster was killing the young KGB agents in his charge.

He stood at the head of the class for at least another minute or two. When he glanced my way, he dismissed me. He smiled at the three serious young men, smiled even more warmly at the young and cute college girls, then looked solemn as he surveyed the rest of the class.

"There is no show without the director," he pronounced in a surprisingly deep voice, his accent not betraying the least hint that he'd been born in the USSR. "There is no film, no play, not even one of those ridiculous sitcoms on television without a director. The director's job is to give life and shape to what the audience sees."

He went on in that vein for some time. It was odd because he hadn't announced which class this was, as if it could be no other class. Nor did he take roll. If I didn't give up taking notes, it was because I was sitting right in front of him. Nonetheless, he figured out pretty quickly that I was not enthralled by his brilliance.

Finally, he paused. "Any questions?"

I raised my hand.

"Yes?" He all but rolled his eyes at my impertinence.

"Is there a syllabus for the course?" I asked.

"Why would you ask that?"

"Because I want to know what the course requirements are so that I can successfully fulfill them."

His glare strongly suggested that I didn't have a chance in hell of doing that. He shrugged.

"If you really need a copy, they are available in the department office." He sighed. "However, the basic requirements are that you direct three scenes, with or without your classmates, and that you read the textbook and apply it. The scenes will be due throughout the quarter with the final scene during finals week." He glared at the class. "Any other questions?"

I was not in the least bit shocked when there weren't any. The only good part about the class, it turned out, was the textbook. It was On Directing, by Harold Clurman, and I really enjoyed reading it. It didn't teach me that much about directing, but I loved the way Clurman bitched about Marlon Brando's inability to speak clearly. I was not a Brando fan. [The only thing worse than your issues with Brando are your issues with Dustin Hoffman, which got significantly worse after this case. - SEH]

Kaspar dismissed us shortly before three p.m. Our assignment for the next class would be to find a scene to direct. The serious students and the young and cute college girls scurried out to follow Kaspar as he left. The others grumbled and tried to figure out who they could get to do what.

Mark, however, plopped into the desk/chair combo next to me.

"What a load of horse manure," he grumbled. Okay. He didn't say manure.

"No kidding." I looked at him. "I'll do your scene if you'll do mine."

Mark shrugged. "Sure. What scene do you want to do?"

"Besides my audition for tomorrow? I have no idea."

"What are you doing for your audition?"

I shrugged. "I don't know about Top Girls."

"You'll just have to do readings for that. Richard's going to be the bitch since Dorfmann wants monologues."

"I know. I'm working on one from Hamlet."

"Hamlet?" Mark grinned and cursed. "Ophelia going crazy?"

"What do you want to bet there will be plenty of those?"

Mark laughed. "So, which one?"

"Gertrude talking about Ophelia's death. 'There is a willow that grows aslant a brook.' What are you doing?"

"Don John's monologue from Much Ado."

"Not Iago?" I grinned.

Mark rolled his eyes. "Everyone will be doing Iago. He's the closest to Richard. Yet, Don John is the one who really gets into the whole being a villain thing."

"Hey, you want to do those as our first scenes?"

Mark looked thoughtful. "Kaspar might go for it. Why don't we work on it now?"

I checked my watch. "Sure. I've got a few minutes."

His Don John was scary. He also had some great notes to give me on my monologue, as well. I was late meeting Sid back at the Humanities meeting, but Sid understood.

We got home well before Nick did, but Sid had papers to grade from the Research class and I had a ton of reading to do. That all got dropped when Nick burst through the front door.

"Mom! Dad!" he hollered. "We had the try-outs for Richard today and I got it!"

"What?" I asked, looking up from the living room couch.

Sid hurried out from the den.

"I'm the Prince of Wales in the play. One of the kids that gets killed. I got the part!"

I bounced up. "Oh, my god, son, that's wonderful!"

Sid laughed. "Somehow, I'm not surprised. Congratulations."

"I'm so proud of you!" I swept him into a warm hug.

We spent the rest of the evening trying to keep Nick off the ceiling. The problem was, we were so happy for him, both Sid and I were on the ceiling, too.

January 14 – 16, 1987

I decided to focus on the Top Girls audition that Wednesday night since I had my first costume shop hours that afternoon. The good news was that Delia Lever, the shop manager, was reasonably impressed with my sewing skills, although there wasn't much to be done yet. Technical rehearsals for the Dance Recital would begin that Friday night, so all the costumes for that were done. They couldn't start making costumes for Top Girls or Richard until those shows were cast, so I was put to work mending costumes from past shows. Even with the audition later, I went home long enough to eat and help clean up after dinner. Nick was still giddy about Richard III, though, and we talked of little else until I had to run to get to the Top Girls audition.

It went well enough, although I couldn't help remembering the production I'd seen with Sid. We'd been undercover then, too. I realized that it had only been three and a half years since that case. Sid was still sleeping around. We had no idea Nick existed. Nick didn't know we did, either. The last thing I wanted was to be married with a kid. I don't think any of us could have imagined us ending up where we are, let alone in the space of three and a half years. And thinking about all of that when I should have been concentrating on reading probably took the edge off my nerves enough that it went as well as it did. It wasn't great, but well enough.

I got through Thursday with a smile from Maggie Leitner and managed not to piss off Earnest Kaspar. I rushed over to Humanities as soon as class let out and worked on catching up on my reading while I waited for Sid to finish his final Western Civ section.

"How are you doing?" he asked as we walked home through the frosty late afternoon.

"I'm a little nervous about tonight." I sighed. "I don't expect much, but I want to do a good job."

"The monologue sounds really good." Sid squeezed my shoulders. "I think you've got it."

We had dinner as soon as Nick got home at five, then Sid insisted I drive back to the campus.

At the audition, Dr. Dorfmann heard all the monologues, then had almost everyone read a scene or two. He asked me to read Anne, then Queen Elizabeth. Casey Limberg, a twenty-ish brunette, looked daggers at me as I read Anne, though. Anne is considered the female lead in the play, and you could tell Casey wanted the part badly.

It was late by the time auditions let out. Sid was already in bed when I got home. He stirred, however, as I slid between the covers.

"What time is it?" he grumbled.

"Almost eleven-thirty. I'm sorry. Dorfmann wouldn't let us go."

He shook his head and woke up completely. "It's okay. Got some interesting intel today. Stinsky was packing to leave when he got killed."

I frowned. "Which means he knew he was a target."

"Or at least, suspected it." Sid shrugged. "Not much to go on, though."

"At the rate we're going, I'll take it."

"I will, too." Sid nuzzled my ear and pulled me close to him.

"You poor thing. You're tired."

"Not that tired." His chuckle took on that nice, lascivious tone. "You?"

I went for it. Neither of us is very good at saying no.

That next morning, as I wandered over the bridge to the performing arts building, I could almost feel the blanket of excitement. The cast lists were up for the two plays, taped on the wall next to the green room. I was not on the Top Girls list, which, truth be told, I expected.

I swelled with pride when I saw Ryan Devereaux's name next to the part of Edward, Prince of Wales. The name next to Anne was Casey Limberg, and I couldn't help smiling. She had really, really wanted the part. Terrence Peterson had been cast as Richard, and I felt a little sad for Mark until I saw that he'd been cast as the First Murderer and Tyndale. Tyndale's monologue about killing the boy princes is incredibly wrenching. What I missed, however, was who was playing Elizabeth.

Mark popped up at my side. "Aren't you going to initial your part?"

"What?"

"You need to sign your initials next to your part to show that you accept it," Mark said.

"What part?" I asked.

Mark laughed loudly. "Yours, dummy. Right there."

His finger landed next to Queen Elizabeth. Next to it read Linda Devereaux.

I gasped. "That's me."

"No kidding." Okay, he didn't say kidding.

"Oh, my god. I got Elizabeth?" I gulped and laughed. "Holy crow!"

I pulled a pen from my daypack and initialed the part, then checked my watch. Sid was well into whatever lecture he was doing for his first section of Western Civ, and I had only about twenty minutes before I needed to be in Voice and Diction. I ran over to the Humanities building and left a note on his office desk.

I was not exactly concentrating during Voice and Diction and totally messed up my exercise. Dorfmann laughed, though. I think he got that I was a little thrown off by the cast list. As the other students left the room, Dorfmann stopped me.

"Congratulations," he said softly.

"Thank you. And... and... and thanks for casting me. This is amazing. Both me and my kid."

His eyebrows lifted. "Your kid?"

"Ryan. He's my son."

"I had no idea."

"What? We have the same last name."

Dorfmann blinked. "Admittedly. And it's not a common one. However, I did not know it until I'd cast the boy, nor was I that conscious of yours." His eyes bore into me. "He doesn't look that much like you."

"That's because he looks like his dad."

"Hm." He cocked his head. "Nor do you seem old enough to have a boy that age."

Technically, I am old enough to have a kid Nick's age, but not by much. That's because I'm only fifteen years older than Nick. Sid is eight years older than me and he's the one who conceived Nick. I'm Nick's second mother because his first mother, Rachel, who gave birth to him, was there first.

I smiled at Dorfmann. "I'm older than I look."

Dorfmann chuckled. "You certainly act that way." His eyes opened wide, and he laughed softly. "This is going to be more fun than I thought. Don't forget. Rehearsals start on the twenty-sixth. They do occasionally run late, and I have to release the children early, so you may want to ask Ryan's father to come by."

"I'll keep that in mind." I smiled. "And thanks again."

I ran straight to the Humanities building from there. Sid looked up from the Research Techniques homework he was grading.

"Hey!" He grinned and got up. "Congratulations."

"Thanks." I giggled excitedly. "I can't believe it."

Sid smiled and hugged me. "I can. I'm so happy for you, honey."

"Thanks." I took a deep breath. "Actually, I've got to get myself back down to earth. Call for the Dance Recital tech rehearsal tonight is six."

"Call?"

"When I have to be there."

"Ah." Sid nodded. "When are you going to eat lunch?"

"Now and between Costuming and Theatre History. Why?"

Sid checked his watch. "We've only got forty-five minutes before our next classes. Why don't you eat lunch with me here, and then I'll pull Nick from the chem lab around four and we can all go to dinner at the Socratic Society at four-thirty."

"I don't think we can afford that."

"I'll put it on the emergency card."

We, as the Devereauxs, had a full collection of credit cards that we, as ourselves, paid the bills on. However, we'd only brought a couple of cards with us. One had a modest balance, and the bill would come to the house in Kansas just in case somebody looked through our mail. That one, however, was strictly for appearances. The other was to pay for emergencies and other stuff that was really needed, but that we couldn't technically afford on Sid's salary.

"We can't afford to do that too often," I said.

"I know." He smiled. "On the other hand, we need to celebrate. Both you and our son have pulled off something amazing." Then he sighed. "I'm also hoping that it might help with the faculty politics if some of those other assholes see me fawning all over my wonderfully talented wife and her fawning all over me."

I couldn't help sniggering. "I don't fawn, and you don't, either."

"True." Sid grinned. "But we do love being in each other's company."

"That we do. Alright. Let's. I think I can get home fast enough to get something on that's nice enough and will still work for the tech rehearsal."

"Not the cashmere dress." Sid sighed. "As much as I love you in it, it might be a bit much."

"Won't work for costume tech, either." I dug one of my sandwiches out of my daypack. "I'll figure something out."

As I hurried to my costume class, I almost ran into Mark Debich in the hall on the first floor of the building.

"Oh, Mark!" I grabbed his arm. "I'm sorry. I was in such shock this morning. Thank you for your help with my monologue. It must have helped."

He grinned. "Thanks. We've still got work to do. At least Kaspar went along with our scenes."

"We still have to get some extra bodies for each," I said, rolling my eyes. "I had no idea being a theatre major was so time consuming."

"Well, I've got Ty Johnson and Perry Willman for Hamlet."

"Think we can talk them into double duty for Much Ado?"

Mark thought. "We should."

"Great." I checked my watch. "Shavings! I've got to run."

I skidded into costume class just after Bev had arrived. After class let out, I ate my second and third sandwiches in the green room while trying to catch up on my theatre history reading. It wasn't easy. Other students wandered in and out, chattering loudly.

"I hope we don't have to stay too late tonight," complained a slender undergrad named Lindsey. I think she was an acting major, but she was in my costume class and was working in the costume shop for the Dance Recital. She sprawled on the sagging, dirty couch.

"With all those wires for the fishes dance?" Tina Monastella said, shoving her long black hair over her shoulder. She was in my acting and directing classes and was going to be dancing in the recital, although it wasn't the fishes dance. She sat cross-legged in one of the easy chairs. "We'll be lucky if we get out before midnight."

"Oh, crap." Okay, Lindsey didn't say crap. "I'll have to call the campus police again to walk me back to the dorms."

"Why?" asked Rita Hornsby, a petite blond grad student focusing on theatre history.

"The campus killer?" Lindsey shrugged and held out her hands, as if it were obvious.

"Killer?" I asked, never mind that I knew exactly which killer they meant.

Rita sighed. "Some cuckoo killed off three students last quarter."

"He's only killing nerds," Tina said. "I mean, it's kinda scary, but doesn't really affect us."

"It's just a pain in the ass waiting for the campus cops to come walk us home at night." Lindsey groaned.

After Theatre History, I ran hell for leather back to the house to get on some nice dress slacks and a pretty blouse and sweater for dinner. I looked at myself in the mirror. The outfit certainly seemed sufficiently circumspect.

When I arrived at the Commons, I was a little surprised to see Raylene in the building's elevator foyer.

She smiled happily. "Well, hello, Linda. It's good to see you."

"Nice to see you, Raylene."

"And what brings you here?"

I smiled. "I'm meeting Charles and Ryan. We're having an early dinner at the Socratic."

The smile on Raylene's face froze. "How sweet of Charles." She sidled up to me and put her arm through mine. "I hope it doesn't reflect poorly on him, though. Not that I believe this..."

"Of course not."

"But men who bring their wives and children to the Socratic are often seen as less than serious about their careers. I think it's silly."

"I'm glad you do." I smiled. "Maybe you and I can help change that idea."

Raylene laughed nervously. "Maybe we can."

She wandered off and left the building. I couldn't figure out why she was there, but let it go. A minute later, Drs. Jeff and Serena Necht came into the foyer, holding hands.

Jeff grinned at me. "Linda, what brings you here?"

"I'm waiting for my husband and son. You?"

"Our weekly dinner at the Socratic." Jeff beamed.

"Oh."

"You look surprised," Serena said.

"Uh, well, something odd I was told just now." I smiled weakly. "My husband is on the history staff."

"History?" Jeff asked.

Serena glared fondly at him. "Yes. You met them a week ago at the faculty reception."

Jeff peered at me.

"My husband is Dr. Charles Devereaux." I smiled. "I'm trying not to flaunt it."

Serena backhanded him in the chest. "Maybe if you'd looked at something besides her boobs that night." She rolled her eyes and smiled at me. "Men."

"Oh!" Jeff grinned and laughed.

I shrugged, feeling my cheeks grow red. "Maybe it's different for theatre faculty."

Jeff and Serena looked at each other, then Serena's eyes narrowed.

"I just saw Raylene Howard leaving here," she said. "What did she tell you?"

I made a face. "Just that men who bring their families to the Socratic are seen as less than serious."

Both Jeff and Serena laughed loudly.

"Carl Howard loves that whole family man thing," Jeff said. "Of course, not enough to bring Raylene to dinner that often."

Serena tittered. "Linda, do not believe a word Raylene says. She hates working faculty wives. Poor thing. The story is that she gave up an amazing fellowship to marry Carl and has been bitter ever since."

"I had no idea she was an academic."

Both Jeff and Serena shrugged, then got on the elevator. Still, it was an interesting perspective on Raylene's character.

Sid and Nick showed up right after. Nick was still overflowing with ecstatic energy. The second he saw me, he ran and darned near knocked me over with the force of his hug.

"We're both in the play!" he hollered.

In sheer joy both at us being in the play and suddenly being big enough, he lifted me off my feet and spun us around.

"Woh! Son!" I yelped, just barely keeping enough presence of mind to not address him by his real name.

Sid laughed. "My son, time to embrace some dignity."

Nick groaned as he released me, then laughed. "And you're playing my mom. This is, like, beyond awesome."

I grinned. "It is."

It turned out to be a perfectly lovely dinner. Sid and I each ordered a glass of bubbly and I, covertly, let Nick have a sip or two. The idea is that we let Nick have a little alcohol in the hopes that he'll learn how to drink responsibly and not see it as forbidden fruit and go off the deep end.

However, it was perilously close to six when I realized I needed to be in the Performing Arts building. I kissed Sid lovingly.

"I've heard rumors that tech rehearsals go really late," I said.

"Give me a call when you're done, and I'll come get you." Sid smiled. "I don't think we need to chance either of us walking home in the middle of the night."

I sighed, but he was right. It wasn't about me being a lone female, unable to protect herself without her big, strong man. It was about being sensible and keeping both of us safe.

I signed in at the costume shop right on time. Lindsey was there and looked at me funny as I hung my parka up on the rack at the back of the room.

"Why did you get so dressed up?" she asked.

"I went to dinner with my husband and kid." I looked around.

We had three other girls working with us: Sandy, Mina, and Hailey. All three were fairly thin, about average height, with brown hair roughly the same shoulder length. Delia Lever came out of her office reeking of cigarette smoke.

"Alright, Linda, I want you on the checkout sheet. The rest of you get the costumes as Linda calls out the name and dance." Delia looked at me. "It's pretty straightforward, but each dancer has to initial that she got the costume, then initial again when it's returned. And do not let anyone check out someone else's costume. Katie Hughes and a couple of the boys are in more than one dance, so don't check out the Rodeo stuff to them until they've brought back their other costumes. Rodeo is the second act, so they'll have plenty of time to get dressed for that. And absolutely no costume goes out to anyone who doesn't have their makeup finished."

The rush to check out costumes began just before seven and ended abruptly just before eight. The music came up through the costume shop speaker, then stopped. Then it started again. Technically, the first act was only supposed to run about an hour and a half. It went considerably longer. The good thing was that as the dancers finished their respective dances, they checked their costumes in.

I still do not know what the music was for the fishes dance, which ended the first act. At least, the title didn't mean anything to me when I eventually saw it on the program. It was weird, though, almost atonal, with five young women dancing and flying through the air in harnesses. Of the four dances that made up the first act, that one took forever to go through. It was almost eleven before that ended.

The ballet Rodeo, with the famous music by Aaron Copland, was the second act. Katie Hughes was dancing the Cowgirl. Tina Monastella danced the Rancher's Daughter, with three other young women as the corps. Five boys, well, young men, were the cowhands. It turned out there was a fast costume change between two of the scenes. The women, except for Katie, just had to change dresses, and that was no problem. Katie had to get out of the same tights made to look like jeans that the guys had on, then get on other tights, a dress, and ballet slippers. Lindsey helped her. The guys also had to get out of the tights made to look like jeans and chaps, and change into shirts and slacks, get string ties tied and jackets on. And it was going to take all the rest of us in the costume shop to help them.

Fortunately, Katie got offstage first. Then the guys all came running off the stage and started peeling off the tights and peeled off their athletic supporters at the same time. Sandy and Hailey shrieked.

"What?" laughed the kid dancing The Roper, a medium-height dirty blond with buffed out shoulders and chest, and... exceptionally gifted in the family jewels department.

I had to assume the other four guys were more normal-sized that way, but it was interesting, and I couldn't help looking at them and then the other kid. I scooped up the athletic supporter from his tights.

"Please put this back on," I said. I could feel the flush on my cheeks and was grateful we were mostly in shadow.

"Impressed?" the kid asked, grinning.

I shook my head. "Trust me. It's not the size of the wand that counts, it's the magic in it."

"You can say that again," Lindsey laughed loudly from where she was closing Katie's dress. "Dom, has she got your number."

Dom snatched his slacks from me as Tracy Schultz, who was stage managing, came striding up.

"Why aren't you guys ready yet?" she demanded.

"We're working out the kinks," I said.

A minute later, the guys were ready. Sandy, Mina, and Hailey were still shrieking and giggling as we went back to the costume shop with the discarded tights and shirts. Once there, Lindsey shook her head and gaped at me.

"You were so cool," she said.

"You just didn't see me blushing." I started checking the pieces in as Lindsey got them ready to be laundered the next day.

"That's Dominic Purslaine, by the way, or, as he likes to call himself, The Stallion." Lindsey paused. "How were you able to stay so cool? I've been a theatre student since high school, and it still gets me."

"My mother-in-law and her boyfriend are nudists," I said.

"But the way you looked at them, as if you didn't care."

I flushed again. "I was just pondering something."

Because of my religious background, Sid is the only man I have ever slept with. Sid, because of his background, growing up among a bunch of communists, beatniks, and eventual hippies, is perfectly comfortable being naked no matter who else is around. So are his aunt Stella and her lover Sy. Sid, Nick, and Sy were the only males I'd seen in the raw. My nephews don't count because the last time I'd seen them naked, they were wearing diapers.

A few months before Sid and I got married, he happened to mention that his family jewels were considered smaller than most guys. Like I was going to know the difference, and I certainly didn't care. Between his incredible popularity back when he'd slept around and, well, the heavy petting we'd been up to at that point, I knew what an amazing lover he was.

It's just that night, when the guys dropped their tights, I realized I was kind of curious about what normal size was. Yeah. Sid is smaller.

It figures, though, that just as I admitted I was pondering something, that's when Sid wandered up to the costume shop.

"Hey, Lover." I grinned as I saw him.

"Hi, sweetie." He bent toward me, then stopped because of the table that had been pulled across the door to keep dancers out of the shop.

"Oh. Here." I pushed the table out of the way. "Come on in."

Sid slid into the shop and kissed me warmly.

"Hey, everyone," I said when I could. "This is my husband, Charles."

Mina shrieked again. "Dr. Devereaux!"

"Uh, Mina, isn't it?" Sid said. "Keeping up on your reading?"

"Yeah." She giggled.

Lindsey eyed Sid appreciatively, then looked at me. The music from the speaker wound to its conclusion. There was a pause.

"Alright, everyone," Tracy Schultz called from somewhere. "Get out of your costumes and get them checked in, then back here for notes. Move it!"

All the girls except Katie showed up together, got their costumes checked in, and hurried off. Dominic showed up as the four guys were finishing up checking in. Sid leaned against a shelving unit next to the door, where he couldn't be seen.

Katie also came up, shaking with fury. She dumped her costumes on the table, turned on Dominic, and screamed an obscene threat if he didn't stop sticking his tongue down her throat during their big kiss at the end of the ballet. Sid silently laughed.

As Katie stormed off, Dominic looked plaintively at me.

"It's like I said," I told him, checking in his costume. "It's the magic in it."

Dom looked pathetic and stalked off. I could hear Sid breaking into laughter next to me.

We were done a couple minutes later, and I offered Lyndsey and the girls a ride back to their dorm. It was a little tight in the car, but fortunately, they all lived in the same building.

"The magic in it?" Sid asked me once we were alone. "Were you referring to the wand line?"

"Yeah. I got a good look when the guys took their tights off for the costume change. Katie was not exaggerating when she said over-sized. Dom thought I should have been impressed. So, I made sure he knew I wasn't." I rubbed the inside of Sid's leg. "After all, you're the guy with the real magic."

Sid laughed, then yawned. "If I can stay awake long enough. Good thing I took a nap after dinner."

January 17 – 20, 1987

Rehearsal that Saturday night went on and on. I will say, the director, Ainsley Winchell, was smart and ran through all the dances except for the fishes dance. She then dismissed all the other dancers, which would have made my life easier, except that the costumes for the fishes dance were a critical part of it since the harnesses for the fly lines were part of the costumes.

"Figure it's going to be another couple hours, at least," Tracy Schultz told us in the costume shop after the other dancers had gone.

"What's the holdup?" I asked.

"What isn't?" Tracy rolled her eyes. "The rigging is really confusing. The dunces holding the ropes can't keep track of when they should pull or lower. The dancers have only been on the ropes since, like last week, so they're not used to them yet."

She ambled off to the theatre lobby to get a smoke in before she had to be backstage. No surprise, smoking was completely forbidden in most of the building. But except for show nights, it was okay to smoke in the lobby. Which made it a popular spot for both theatre students and faculty, many of whom smoked like an all-day barbecue. I called Sid. It wasn't yet ten o'clock.

"We're going to be here for a while," I told him, then dropped my voice. "However, I've found a way to keep track of what's going on and a place where we can get some privacy, if you'd like to enjoy some lovemaking then go straight to sleep when we get home."

"I'm on my way."

I set up my transmitter in my daypack so that it picked up what was coming through the speaker in the costume shop and pulled out my small flashlight. As I slid the earpiece receiver to the transmitter in my ear, Sid showed up in the hallway. I made sure the other girls didn't see him, then we slid up the hallway to the stairs, and up to the third floor. I pulled the pass key I had for the entire building from my jeans pocket and let us into the Costume Warehouse.

It was not really a warehouse. Just a really, really large room with a two-story ceiling and racks and racks of clothing, accessories, and all sorts of costume pieces, like crowns and prosthetics and just about anything someone would wear in a play. Delia Lever had explained that they never threw anything away unless it was completely destroyed, and a good half of everything in there had been remade at least once, most of it multiple times.

I left the lights off. I didn't want anyone seeing one under the doorsill and come investigating. Sid and I started necking almost immediately, but then I switched on my penlight and pulled him further into the room. I could hear the speaker downstairs, and while it was possible that the rehearsal would let out early, it sure didn't seem like it would. There was a battered wing-back chair next to an equally battered desk. Sid slid into the chair. We were fully engaged when we heard the door open. The lights turned on. Sid kept going (he doesn't stop for anything), but we both had to hold our breath so that we didn't make any noise.

Whoever had come in paced in the doorway for a few minutes, then the door opened again. All we could hear was the low thrum of a voice, at first. It sounded like it was coming from the doorway, but it was hard to tell.

"You're wasting your time," said Earnest Kaspar. His voice came from deeper in the warehouse and I could just see the line of his hair through the floor to ceiling shelving.

The first voice mumbled something.

"They will not let you have the career you want. Trust me, I know."

The door slammed shut. Kaspar cursed and then the door opened and shut. I had to assume he had left, which was a good thing because Sid and I were both at the point where we were going to make noise whether we wanted to or not.

Sid chuckled when we were done. "So, did the threat of discovery enhance the experience?"

"Not really." I gasped and blinked. "Thank you, though. It was nice of you to come over."

"I was happy to, and thank you, too." He softly kissed me. "And at least we've got an option for any more late nights at school. Not counting my office, of course."

"Anywhere we can," I said. "What do you think about what we just overheard?"

"What's to think? Somebody was having a conference of some sort."

"The one voice was Earnest Kaspar."

Sid mused. "That puts an interesting wrinkle on it." He shook his head. "He must be coming up here to meet with his finishing students. I hope whoever is going after them isn't watching this room."

"I hope so, too."

"We'll have to see if our friend David can spend some late nights practicing up here."

I turned out the lights as we left. We went downstairs, and I was able to get cleaned up quickly. Still, Leslie looked at me, then saw Sid, and she began laughing. I flushed and rolled my eyes. Mina, who was still in idol worship mode, just smiled beatifically at Sid and completely missed that he ignored her.

"How many sweet young things like her do you have in your classes?" I whispered in his ear.

He winced. "Roughly sixty percent. It's a little annoying."

"Why?"

"They're idiots. If they'd stop drooling, they might actually learn something."

I grinned. "That's too bad. On the other hand, I feel for those poor, misbegotten little fools. They may dream, but they will never know."

I squeezed his backside, and he laughed loudly.

We did not get home until after one that morning. By the next morning, we both overslept and just barely got Nick up and ourselves functioning in time to get to mass. We'd made our weekly phone calls the day before, but I still had laundry to finish. Not that I'd have the chance right away.

Back when I was still working on my undergrad degree and my master's (which I hold in English Literature, with an emphasis on Shakespeare) my goal had been to become an English professor. I'd initially had to put my PhD program on hold while I made some money, so I'd taught for a year at a community college, then got laid off thanks to budget cuts. A year later, I ran into Sid in a bar after ditching a blind date and the rest, well, happened.

Then the case in Wisconsin happened. Both Sid and I were undercover, but my cover was as an English professor, and as part of that cover, I set up something I'd done back when I was teaching for real, namely Off-Campus Office Hours. Basically, I let all my students know that I'd be at such-and-such a place from this time to that, bought some pizzas and drinks, and let them come and ask questions and get to know each other. Before Sid, it was a great opportunity to help kids that would not show for regular office hours. In Wisconsin, it also provided a visible reason to connect to the rest of our team.

Sid had decided to do the same and invited Randall and Irene to join us. After all, Irene and I were old friends, and Randall was getting to be an even better one, thanks to Nick.

We landed at a nearby Italian restaurant called Angelo's that served beer and wine, and ordered three large pizzas, a pitcher of beer, and a pitcher of soda. I ordered a glass of white wine that turned out to be just barely drinkable.

Mina and four other sweet young things were the first to show, then LeShawn Pile and Karen Crombie. I knew Karen as Kathy Deiner, a tall woman with dark chocolate skin. She'd taken to wearing a wig with a straightened do, and was also wearing a full, flowing, and brightly colored top over a full skirt.

Karen sat next to me, with Irene on her other side.

"How are you doing?" I asked softly.

"Just some morning sickness."

One of the bigger problems we had when setting up our team was how to explain why all six of us had suddenly disappeared at the same time to the rest of our friends in our parish back home. Kathy's pregnancy had proven useful. While they had told their families about the photo tour, she and Jesse simply left the parish and go to another parish where there were more Blacks. After all, they wanted their kids to know their culture. They were also selling their condo so that they could buy a house in Baldwin Hills, an area known for its upscale Black population.

I was a little surprised to see Terrence Peterson come in, and he was even more surprised to see me.

"What are you doing here?" he asked.

"Following my husband around." I shrugged. "You?"

"I'm taking Dr. Devereaux's Research class. It's my first quarter as a grad student." He looked around the table and frowned. "Who's your husband?"

I laughed. "Dr. Devereaux. This is our son Ryan. Honey, come meet Terrence."

Nick got up from where he was sitting next to Sid and grinned.

"Hi," said Terrence. "Actually, I prefer Terry. Why does Ryan Devereaux sound so familiar?"

"He's playing the young Prince of Wales," I said. "Ryan, Terry is playing Richard the Third."

"Awesome!" Nick laughed. "This is so cool."

"So, Ryan's your kid?" Terry looked at us. "Funny. You don't look very much alike."

"I look like my dad." Nick jerked his thumb toward his father.

"Oh."

Sid suddenly noticed that Terry was there. "Hey, Terry, what's up?"

"Just trying to figure out some term paper topics." Terry went over and sat next to Sid.

"Dad, he's playing Richard the Third."

Sid nodded. "That's right. You said you were going for your master's in acting."

"Back up so I can teach."

"Wise decision. Now, how can I help you?"

Nancy and Dave Lemon showed next, followed by more sweet young things. Sid had told me he'd picked up the mail from home from our friend while I'd been at the rehearsal the night before. Since Nick was bouncing around the table, he got the two envelopes we had to the right couples.

Nancy was Vietnamese, and we knew her as Esther Nguyen. Her husband, Dave, was really Frank Lonergan. Frank had dyed his hair red and put on glasses. Esther had settled for cutting her hair extra, extra short and wore glasses, as well. They'd told their families and everyone at church that they were thinking of getting their master's degrees and wanted to get away some place cheaper to live than Los Angeles to test out whether grad school was a good idea or not.

Esther cursed relentlessly about the cold weather.

"She's not used to it," said Frank, laughed. He's originally from the Chicago area.

I eventually checked my watch and saw that it was getting close to call time.

"I've gotta take off," I sighed. "Mina, can I give you a ride back to school?"

"How are we getting home, Mom?" Nick asked.

"We'll give you guys a ride," said Randall, joining the conversation for the first time that afternoon.

School was technically within walking distance of Angelo's, but everyone was moving in packs, it seemed. It had been a while since the Campus Killer had struck, still, no one wanted to take any chances.

Mina accepted the ride to school but was downcast as she got into the car with me.

"He's married," she sighed.

"Yep."

"Married and with a kid."

"Yep. And the kid isn't even fourteen, so hands off there, too."

She looked at me. "He is so gorgeous, and really smart, too."

"He is, at that."

"We had our first quiz on Friday." She made a face. "I don't think I did very well."

"I'll tell you a secret. You might do better if you listened to the lecture and did the reading."

I could see her trying not to roll her eyes.

Lindsey was surprised to see Mina and I walk in together.

"Linda gave me a ride," Mina said.

Lindsey laughed. "So, does this mean you're not going to disappear when things get slow tonight?"

I shrugged. "I might take a walk or two around the building. As for whether or not Charles will show, we'll see."

I took a walk or two around the building during the first three dances and discovered there was a decided problem with the place, especially in terms of my real purpose in being there. It seemed like there were people around constantly, and it wasn't just faculty working late. If anything, those people left early. It was the students who roamed the halls. Most of them were concentrated on the end of the building where the two theater spaces were, and were obviously working on the Dance Recital. But more than one classroom had students in them, mostly working on scenes.

I went ahead and got into the Nechts' shared office and did a quick search. There was nothing there to trigger more interest. No hidden porn, no strange letters. Jeff Necht's interest in my chest the week before, notwithstanding, he seemed to be quite loyal to his wife and focused on his students.

It was a little nerve-wracking sliding out of the office. I listened at the door, but given how soundproof the offices were, I couldn't be one-hundred percent certain that there was no one in the hall when I slid out. There wasn't anybody. That didn't mean that would always be the case.

One thing I did not do, and I was glad I didn't, was assume that the fishes dance would take forever. I returned to the costume shop just as the dance started. The music continued and didn't stop. At the end, the five of us listened.

"Alright. That looked good," called the choreographer's voice. "Get your costumes checked in and notes in the ballet studio."

The five of us in the costume shop didn't exactly cheer, but we were relieved.

The ballet went smoothly, as well, and I was home before ten-thirty. Sid was thrilled and made sure I knew it.

Tuesday, however, we were not thrilled at all. We were pissed off. We'd gotten the bill that had most worried me, and it turned out I had good reason to worry.

"It's three times what I budgeted for," I wailed, waving the fuel oil bill around. "We can't afford this!"

Sid grabbed the paper from me and cursed. "Why is it so expensive?"

"Because you keep turning the heat up."

"It's cold in here."

I glared at him. "I know. But we agreed we were going to put on sweaters."

"We've got sweaters on."

I looked at the thermostat. "How are you cold? It's seventy degrees in here."

"It's not that warm in the den. Our son has three blankets and an afghan on his bed, and he's complaining."

"You would never have survived my parents' place. If the temperature went up over sixty-seven during the winter, we'd get our fannies tanned."

"We're not at your parents' place. And it's ridiculous that I have to wear earmuffs and mittens inside my house."

I grabbed the bill back. "Fine. Then what are we going to cut to pay for this?"

"I don't know. Maybe you could try eating a little less."

"Our son, too?"

Sid glared at me. "He's a growing boy. What's your excuse?"

"High metabolism." I sniffed. "And what are you going to give up? Lunch at the Socratic?"

"Those are important meetings that build our cover, plus give me a chance to consider suspects. You haven't done a whole hell of a lot of investigating."

"We've barely been here two weeks. I'm establishing my cover. And I'm trying to search offices in a building that does not shut down at night. I dare you to try."

Sid sighed. "We're getting off track here."

I sniffed as I looked at the bill. "We're going to have to use the emergency card."

"I'm afraid so." Sid cursed. "At least we have it." He sighed deeply. "And I'll turn down the thermostat. We can probably get away with sixty-five overnight, too."

"We'll need to make one more emergency purchase. It is cold in that den. Why don't we see if we can get a small space heater? That should help."

"I sure hope so." Sid looked at me, haplessly. "I'm sorry I got on your case about the food."

"Thanks. I'll try not to worry so much about the money."

Nick hurried into the house, slamming the front door.

"Are you guys done fighting yet?"

We looked at him, suddenly terrified.

"What did you hear?" Sid asked slowly.

"Just yelling." Nick shrugged, then grew afraid. "I couldn't tell about what. Come on. You guys fight all the time."

I swallowed. "But we don't usually have to worry about keeping a cover intact with a nosy neighbor listening outside our windows."

"She hasn't since that first time, has she?" Sid asked.

I grabbed my boots from the space next to the door. "I haven't seen any tracks, but I haven't looked in a while."

There hadn't been any more snow for several days, and the drifts all around the house were free of footprints.

"That was close," Sid sighed as he made dinner.

"I guess we're going to have to take our fights to the basement."

Sid and I were still feeling a little raw that evening, but he turned down the thermostat, and didn't groan too loudly when I turned it down still further for overnight. We'd explained to Nick about the fuel oil bill, and he reluctantly agreed that it was better to conserve.

Later, once we were sure he was asleep, Sid got frisky, as he often did after a fight. Okay, I was pretty frisky, too. I was glad Nick had his headphones on.

The next morning, there were tracks under our bedroom windows.

January 22 – 29, 1987

Thursday night, the Dance Recital officially opened. The air outside the costume shop was electric, and the noise of an audience filtered through the costume shop speaker.

"What's she doing back here?" Delia growled and left the shop.

I walked to the door and looked out. Raylene Howard was headed toward the backstage area of the main theater when Delia caught up with her. I hid in the shop as Delia escorted Raylene toward the front of the building.

"I understand you're concerned," Delia said soothingly, "But it really isn't safe for the dancers to have audience members wandering around back here."

Delia returned to the shop, rolling her eyes.

"What's the witch after now?" Lindsey asked.

"She heard there's been some nudity backstage and wanted to be sure we were protecting the students."

Lindsey groaned. "Why does she do stuff like that?"

Delia shrugged. "From what I've heard, the college president's wife is worried about school morals. It's gotten worse with that killer on the loose. Apparently, enrollment this quarter went down, with a bunch of kids transferring out."

"I'd heard Raylene is best friends with Isabel Lovegood," I said.

"Who's Isabel?" Lindsey asked.

"The college president's wife," said Delia. She shook her head. "Campus politics. The only thing worse is working in a professional theater." She sighed, then bit her lip. "Oh, I'm sorry, Linda. I forgot you're a faculty wife, too."

"That doesn't mean I enjoy campus politics," I said. "And I am no friend of Raylene Howard. I just have to be nice to her since her husband is my husband's boss."

Tracy's voice came over the speaker, calling the dancers for the first dance to the backstage area. Several minutes later, the audience chatter stilled, then the music poured out. Sid and Nick were somewhere in the audience, partly out of interest and partly because of more campus politics. It turned out Carl Howard and University President Sebastian Lovegood were big supporters of the arts, especially if they attracted a significant paying audience. Fortunately, Collins' theatre department did, pulling subscription members from Topeka and even Kansas City.

I had dressed in my nice blouse and dark slacks. There would be a reception in the other theater for subscription members, faculty, and the dancers after the performance. Crew members weren't supposed to go, but I was a faculty wife, and should have been in the audience.

In fact, by the time the Dance Recital was finished, and the costumes checked in, the party was in full swing on the tiny stage. Mimi Dearing made a point of sliding up to me before I could find Sid or Nick.

"Why didn't I see you earlier?" she asked, simpering.

"I was backstage." I smiled. "I'm taking a costume class this quarter and it's required to work a crew."

"Taking a class?" Mimi's eyes rose.

Raylene and a tall, stately woman with dark gray hair, joined us.

"You're taking classes?" Raylene asked. "Are you sure that's wise?"

"Well, it is part of the deal I have with Charles."

"Charles?" asked the stately woman.

"I'm so sorry," said Raylene. "Isabel, this is Linda Devereaux. Her husband is the visiting history professor. Linda, this is Isabel Lovegood, our president's wife."

Isabel's eyes flitted over to where Sid and Nick were chatting with Dominic Purslaine, of all people, and she gazed appreciatively. I shook her hand.

"It's a pleasure meeting you, Mrs. Lovegood."

She wrenched her gaze back to me. "Oh, Isabel, please. Sebastian and I truly try to keep a pleasant and friendly atmosphere here at Collins."

"But taking classes," Raylene said.

"Oh, that was Charles' idea." I smiled. "You see, I supported him and Ryan while he got his degrees, and the only reason he let me do that was if I promised to do my graduate work when he got a post. So, I'm working on undergrad prerequisites for my master's. Charles insisted."

That took some air out of them. Nice wives that they were, they couldn't question me doing what my husband wanted me to, even if it was something they didn't approve of.

"Will you ladies excuse me?" Smiling, I nodded at Sid and Nick. "I haven't had a chance to say hi to Charles or Ryan yet."

I went over to where Sid and Nick were still chatting with Dominic. Actually, Nick and Dom were doing most of the chatting. Dom was also in Richard III, playing both Clarence and Richmond, which I thought was going to be a little awkward since there is one spot where the two characters are on stage together.

"Hey, Lover," I said happily.

"Hey, yourself, my beloved." Sid grinned and gave me a delicious little kiss.

"Mom!" Nick plowed into me with a hug. "This is Dominic. He's going to be in the play, too."

"I know." I looked at Dom. "How long have you been dancing, Dom?"

"Since grade school," he said. "I didn't really start ballet, though, until high school, which is too late if you're going to join a big company. The program here is good because it does have a strong emphasis on ballet, but that's so you can do more as a dancer on Broadway or other theatre."

"Yes, I'd heard that." I leaned into Sid's body as he slid his arm around my shoulders.

Dom looked at me a little funny, but then Katie Hughes came up to say hi, ostensibly to me, but I could tell she wanted to meet Sid. Sid squeezed me and we laughed about it later that night.

That Sunday, Irene and Kathy were already seated together and chatting like old friends when Sid, Nick, and I showed up at Angelo's for Off-Campus Office Hours. Randall had stayed home.

"He's working on his first midterm exams," Irene said.

I groaned. "I've got at least two coming up, and one project."

Jesse came in with Mina and her friends. Terry Peterson followed with one of the other grad students in the Research class. Esther and Frank came in as well.

"We probably shouldn't stay long," Esther told us, punctuating her rant with curse words. "There's a big blizzard coming in tonight. The weatherman says a couple feet of snow, at least. We're going to be trapped. I hope you have lots of extra food and toilet paper."

Frank patted her hand. "We'll be fine, sweetheart. This is not the first blizzard I've lived through."

Terry laughed. He was getting to like Esther. I wasn't surprised. The two were amazingly good at dirty double-entendres. Sid had backed off, trying to keep the family man image.

Nick saw to discreetly getting the mail distributed while Irene, Kathy, and I chatted.

"The condo closed last week," Kathy whispered to me, after looking at the particularly thick envelope she had. "How do we get the paperwork returned?"

"We'll call our friend," I whispered back. "If this blizzard is as bad as they say, he'll probably be stuck here if he hasn't flown out already."

Right before five, I asked Mina if she wanted a ride to school. We had an earlier call time because the show would start an hour earlier that night. Irene volunteered to take Sid and Nick home. When Mina and I got to school, I pulled a loaded laundry basket from the trunk.

"What's that?" asked Mina.

"I've just got some ironing to do."

What I had was a whole bunch of Sid's dress shirts. They were all cotton, although not the fine Egyptian cotton Sid usually wears, and had come out of the dryer reasonably wrinkle-free. However, Sid really likes a nice, stiffly starched collar, cuffs, and front, which meant I needed to iron them. Sid had volunteered to do it, but I'm a lot better at ironing than he is. While I couldn't get the collars as stiff as he preferred with the spray starch I'd been using, I could still do it better than he could.

Things were going smoothly enough with the Dance Recital that I was able to get most of the shirts done. I would have gotten all of them done, but Delia saw what I was doing, asked about it, and showed me how to use the really heavy liquid starch.

"I may as well show you," Delia said. "We've got both Top Girls and Richard costumes to work on, and there are starched wimples for both shows."

"Goody, goody, gumdrops," I grumbled.

Nonetheless, Sid was ecstatic when he saw his freshly ironed and starched shirts when I got home right around ten.

"You are amazing." He held me close to him. "These are perfect!"

I pulled away somewhat reluctantly and put the shirts in our closet.

"I'm glad you're happy," I said with a smile. "However, I missed the team part of our meeting today and I'd really like to know what's going on."

"Oh. Right." Sid pulled me close to him again, then got us sat down on the edge of the bed. "Frank has been hitting the practice rooms most nights of the week but hasn't seen anything. Jesse is thinking about doing some surveillance on Mimi. He just has to figure out how. Kathy got us a profile on Steve Weber."

"Who's he?"

"One of the other history guys." Sid shrugged. "He seems to be the least invested in his marriage and has even joked about getting violent with his wife."

"That doesn't make him a rogue agent out to get KGB agents."

"No kidding. But the tendency toward violence might be a hint."

"It might. Do we have any background on Mimi yet? Oh, and I'd love to find out if that story about Raylene giving up a fellowship to marry Carl is true."

"Damn. Forgot to ask about Raylene." Sid looked at me and sighed. "I wish you'd been able to stay."

"I wish I had been able to." I frowned. "It's tough getting things this way."

The wind began whistling around the house. I looked out the window only to see white flakes dancing sideways.

"I think the blizzard is here."

Sid looked at the window and had to agree.

Nick somehow slept through the howling of the wind but was awake first that next morning. The snow was still coming down heavily.

"Mom! Dad! Check this out!"

I groaned and put my pillow over my head. Sid got up and grabbed a robe. It had gotten pretty cool in the house.

"Don't let him go outside," I said. "It looks like white-out conditions."

"I'll take your word for it. Can I put the heat on?"

"Please."

"I'll get the radio on, too. Irene told me last night that they'll broadcast a list of closures, if there are any."

I yawned. "Good odds."

Sure enough, the radio announcer droning out the schools and other closures included the Evelyn Casey Educational Center and all of Collins State University.

"What's that mean?" Nick asked.

"It means we're not going anywhere today," I replied, wrapping my heavy terry-cloth robe even more tightly around me.

"Cool." As much as Nick liked his current school, a day off was always welcome. "Hey, maybe we can have a snowball fight."

"Not until the snow stops," I told him. "The way it looks out there right now, you could get five steps away from the door and get totally lost."

Nick was impressed, but, fortunately, he believed me. Sid and I spent the day getting caught up on our respective schoolwork. Nick finished all the homework he had from his school back home before noon and pronounced himself bored. I finally handed him my Complete Works of Shakespeare and put him to work reading all of Richard the Third.

Shortly after noon, Tracy Schultz called.

"I'm the Richard stage manager," she grumbled. "Rehearsals are canceled for tonight."

"I'm not surprised." I said.

"I'll call tomorrow if they're still canceled."

The next day, we were still snowbound, which meant everything was still closed and rehearsals were canceled. It had stopped snowing by mid-day, but there was so much snow, the snowplows didn't get to us until almost dark. Sid, Nick, and I had taken turns shoveling all afternoon, only to have the plows bury our driveway again. Gasping, we took turns going at it. I fervently prayed we'd be clear the next morning. We were all getting a little on the punchy side.

It was still dark when Sid nudged me awake.

"What?" I groaned.

"Our son is already in the shower. Apparently, it's on the radio that everything has re-opened."

I couldn't get out much more than a mumble. We were at the school by seven. I'm still not sure why I went over to the theatre department, but I discovered something. The place was as close to deserted as I'd ever seen it. I sighed deeply. I am not a morning person. But this was my area. It was still close enough to eight that I decided to wait on any searches.

The Fitness Center was open and somewhat deserted. Sid was already on one of the treadmills. I got on the one next to him. He finished his hour before I did and went to shower and dress. We crossed paths and kissed as he left to go to his office, and I headed for the showers. It was starting to look like a normal Wednesday.

It wasn't entirely, but that was mostly because Nick was on the ceiling. Richard rehearsals were to start that night at six-thirty. Sid had dinner ready at five on the dot. I was grateful. It was one thing that felt truly normal. At home, the three of us eat dinner together most nights. In Kansas, we'd had even more opportunity to stay home since dinner out was a luxury and my schedule had gotten so full.

Sid drove us to school that night and went to his office to work on writing up his Research midterm and grading the Western Civ ones from that day. He was giving all his classes two midterm exams, as were most of my teachers. The Richard cast gathered in the tiny director's theater that we'd also be using as our rehearsal space. There were around twenty of us, plus Dr. Dorfmann and Tracy Schultz.

Now, if you're going to do a full production of Richard III, with every line in the original play and each actor having only one role, then you're looking at a five-hour play with a cast of over sixty people. Like most Shakespeare produced in this day and age, the script had been cut down and several characters eliminated. Other characters were also double cast, such as Clarence and Richmond, who I'd already noted, were both going to be played by Dominic Purslaine. Mark Debich was also double cast as a murderer and Tyrell, of the wrenching monologue about killing the young princes.

The five female roles, no surprise, were mostly intact and none of us were double cast. I sat in the little lecture seat next to Casey Limberg, who had gotten the part she'd wanted, that of the unlucky Anne.

"I was so mad when I heard you read," she told me softly while the photocopied scripts and rehearsal schedules were distributed. Someone had gone to an awful lot of trouble and had re-typed the entire play as it would be produced. "I was so sure you'd get Anne."

"I'm glad I didn't, then," I said.

Dr. Dorfmann got up and stood at a small podium. "To quote the Bard in another play, 'Is all our company met?'"

"Everyone's here," Tracy said.

"Well, then, we are looking at Richard the Third, one of Shakespeare's greatest villains, perhaps only eclipsed by Iago in Othello. Before anyone objects." Dorfmann grinned at me. "I think we should remember that we are not dealing with the historical King Richard the Third, who probably got his evil reputation because of this play. We are dealing with the image of him as preferred by the Elizabethans. Richard is called a spider multiple times in the text, and that is the image I have chosen as our touchstone. He ensnares all the other characters in his web of deceit and is eventually ensnared by his own deeds. Even though we are not dealing with a historical Richard, I am putting the play in its Fifteenth Century setting. We will use dance as a visual element, hence Ms. Hughes will be joining us to choreograph our other six women. There will also be a musical element, as well, and I am working that out with the music department. Once we get blocked, we will have several rehearsals with our musicians. I do have some bad news. Normally, we will have Saturdays and Sundays off from rehearsals until tech. However, thanks to our recent inclement weather, we will work this weekend. I know some of you have conflicts thanks to the Dance Recital, but we will work around them. Now, our first task is to do our read-throughs. Language is a key element of Shakespeare, so we will focus on that tonight and tomorrow night and however often we need to. Now, let us begin. Terry?"

Terry took a deep breath, and his voice filled the space from the front row. It was clear why he'd gotten the role. I had brought my knitting and Nick had brought his. It was a good thing. I could see Nick getting a little antsy.

I was also thrilled when we were done by nine-forty-five. The production would probably run somewhat longer, but the read-through clocked in at just under two-hours, not counting a couple breaks. Nick practically ran to his father's office. Sid was pleased, too, though a little bleary-eyed.

"How did you stay on top of your grading in Wisconsin?" he asked after Nick had gone to bed. "I'm not handing out a third of what you assigned us, and I feel like I'm drowning. And those midterms." He cursed. "The handwriting is impossible, and none of them can write a coherent thought. I should have made it all multiple guess."

"Instead, you asked two essay questions and a bunch of short answers."

"At least, they're mostly getting the salient points." He sighed.

The next morning, I went in early to the costume shop. Delia Lever was in a panic. It was getting awfully close to the Top Girls tech rehearsals and there was still a lot to be done on those costumes, plus the Richard costumes were going to take a lot of work. If I got there by nine, Delia would be able to get me measured for my costume, I'd be able to measure Terry for his and possibly get the plaster cast made of his back so that she could create a hump for him since he would need to rehearse with it. I'd bring Nick by the next day after school and before Lab Rats to get measured.

Terry was waiting for me, and pretty comfortable being measured, wearing a t-shirt and tights since he wouldn't be able to wear traditional underwear. He stood patiently while I measured all his body parts and filled out the form. Delia had the plaster of Paris ready by the time I was done. Terry laid down in the ooze, and we waited while it set, which it did quickly. He got up and there was a big block of plaster attached to his back.

"It's not coming off," I grumbled. "I'm going to have to cut your t-shirt off."

"No!" Terry yelped. Fear shone in his eyes.

"I'll get you a new one," I said. Delia had left the shop for a cigarette break and the two of us were alone.

Terry glanced back at his shoulder, and I suddenly realized what the problem was, the tattoo of a swastika on his shoulder.

"Um, Terry, remember right before school started, we saw each other in the Health Center? You had that horrible cough?"

He frowned, then nodded.

"Well, as they were taking me in, the nurse in your treatment cubicle opened the curtains and I saw what was on your shoulder."

Terry swallowed and closed his eyes. "I don't believe in that. I really don't." He looked at me pleadingly. "I come from this small town in southern Indiana. There were a lot of Klan people there. One night, I got drunk with some friends. Or guys I thought were friends. We went to a tattoo parlor. I don't know why they helped us since we were all underage. I passed out, and they did that to me. They thought it was funny. And it's permanent."

"Have you seen a dermatologist? I've heard it's pretty painful, but it's possible to remove something like that."

"I'd like to." He sighed. "Maybe I'll ask them at the Health Center."

"Alright. Let's get this cut off and you can get your shirt back on before anyone else comes in."

It didn't take long, and Terry gave me a big hug for being so nice about it. Later, in Beginning Directing, I watched Mark do the scene I was directing him in for the rest of the class. Kaspar ripped it to shreds with an extended lecture on respecting Shakespeare by treating it honestly. Whatever that meant.

I was not in a good mood at dinner, and it didn't help that dinner ran late. Sid took us back to school again and again hid in his office grading exams and Research Techniques homework. Nick and I rushed to the directing room straight from the car and got there just barely in time.

Many of the students paid for lockers in the dressing rooms to hold their coats and other stuff. I hadn't because I'm cheap and I had a place to drop my parka and other stuff, namely, Sid's office. That night, I laid the coat down in the back row of the directing room, next to another parka that looked an awful lot like mine. Nick kept his parka next to him. At the end of the read-through, I had to stay behind to work out when I was going to be at rehearsal over the next few days since I was also working costumes for the Dance Recital that was still on. I was hardly the only one who had to. So, I sent Nick on ahead to get his father and said that I'd meet them at the car.

As soon as I worked out the times, I grabbed what I thought was my parka and hurried out of the back of the building to cross the small field behind to the parking lot.

The blow came out of nowhere. I was in the middle of open space, and I swear I did not hear anyone crunching through the snow behind me. After landing face-down in the snow, I felt a heavy hand pushing my face down into the drift.

I tried to roll over, but the hold on me was firm.

"Linda!" called somebody from the performing arts building.

The hold released and the next thing I knew, I could get up. Mark Debich came running up.

"Are you alright?"

Gasping, I nodded. "Thank God. Did you see who that was?"

"No." He looked around. "But he must have hidden behind that drift." He pointed, then helped me up. "You have my coat."

I looked down. "Oh. It's almost like mine."

Sid and Nick ran up.

"Honey? Are you alright?"

"Fine." I took my parka from Mark and handed him his. "Mark, are you walking home?"

He pointed at the lot. "I have a car."

"We'll walk you to it," said Sid. "Apparently, there's some madman on the loose."

"I know." Mark swallowed. "He was coming for me."

"You? What makes you so sure?" I asked.

"I can't say." Mark sighed. "I don't know who the Campus Killer is, but I know why he's attacking. I can't say why that is, but I do."

"We should call the police," Sid said.

"No." Mark shook his head. "It won't do any good. We didn't see anything."

Sid disagreed and took me back inside the building to call. Mark disappeared.

Sid and I went around and around, speculating about what had happened. We'd called the cops because we needed to look like civilians. The cops had been darned evasive, but we still were pretty certain that I'd been attacked by the killer. It fit too closely to what had happened to Rod Stinsky. Then there was Mark's assessment that he was the target. It wasn't conclusive by any stretch, but it sure seemed like there was at least one more KGB agent doing his finishing training than we'd known about.

The other thing that bothered me, though, was Terry. Just that morning, I'd revealed that I knew his secret.

Now, I knew that White Supremacists were not necessarily anti-Communist. We knew of one, specifically, that was perfectly happy talking to the Soviets about taking down the U.S. government. On the other hand, the timing was suspicious, at best, and no one had seen Terry since rehearsal had let out.

Then there was that report on Dr. Steve Weber that Sid had gotten from Karen the week before. There wasn't much to go on. Weber had no criminal record and no visible connection to anyone in the Intelligence Community, nor did his wife, Susan. He had a father who was being treated for paranoid schizophrenia. The older man was convinced that the KGB had infiltrated the greater Kansas City area and was poisoning the water there. It didn't seem likely that Weber shared his father's delusions, but even if he didn't, he could have similar feelings about the Soviets and the KGB.

Finally, that Friday afternoon, I happened to overhear Jeff Necht complaining that Raylene Howard had been snooping around the building the night before.

I was surprised Saturday afternoon when we got a phone call from Raylene herself.

"It's all over school that you met up with the Campus Killer the other night." Raylene sounded excited.

"We don't know for sure," I said. "The police wouldn't say."

"It must have been terrifying," she said. "How did you stand it?"

"It was scary, to be sure. How did you hear about it? I didn't really tell anyone."

"Well, darling, I'm on campus every day."

"I heard someone saw you in the Performing Arts building that night."

Raylene tittered. "Oh, I might have been. Carl has a late class on Tuesdays and Thursdays. I sometimes go over there to wait for him to get out."

"Did you see anything unusual in that field behind Performing Arts?"

"I'm so sorry, but I didn't."

"Oh, dear. I was hoping. Raylene, I'm so sorry, but I really don't want to talk about what happened. It just makes me more scared. I hope you understand."

"Of course. I'm glad that you're alright."

I was not thrilled to find out when I got to the costume shop that the story of my encounter with the Campus Killer was, in fact, making the rounds. The interesting thing was that Mark's involvement had completely escaped notice.

Delia was cool about me taking off for rehearsal. She just wanted me back in time to help with the Rodeo fast change. I'd already talked to Dr. Dorfmann about that one. He wasn't thrilled, but he was already blocking later scenes because Dominic was in the ballet and not available.

One of the scenes we blocked that night was one of Nick's two scenes. I'd explained to Nick the whole blocking process, which was going line by line through the script and the director telling us how we'd move on stage. I even showed him the usual shorthand. Dr. Dorfmann was impressed by how fast Nick picked it up and I couldn't help but be proud.

Tyler Noble, the kid playing the younger of the two doomed princes, had it down already, even though he was only eleven. But then, this was hardly the first play Tyler had done. The kid even had a little bit of an attitude, and part of me really wanted to do something about it. Sid was hanging around to supervise Nick while I helped with the fast change for the ballet and did not have nice things to say about Tyler's mother, who was also there. Dorfmann was firm that any underage actor had to have at least one parent at the rehearsal at the same time. [Tyler's mother was a piece of work. She had his entire Hollywood career mapped out. I was not surprised when he showed up on that kid's show that everyone was so excited about, and even less when he crashed and burned a few years later. - SEH]

Sunday, we went to mass, then eventually Off-Campus Office Hours. Mina didn't show for some reason, although some of the other sweet young things did. Kathy/Karen and Jesse/LeShawn didn't show, either.

"We'll be at your place tonight," Esther/Nancy whispered to me. "We thought it would look funny if we all showed up every week, and we've got something for you."

It was just as well. I had to take off early for the final performance of the Dance Recital, and Sid was going to have to leave soon after to take Nick to rehearsal since they were blocking the last scenes that night and I wasn't in any of them. Which meant there wouldn't be any time for a team meeting after all the civilians had gone.

There had been a cast party for the recital the night before, and I was not surprised to see that half the dancers were not as lively as usual. Dominic was reportedly suffering a monster hangover, not to mention a broken heart.

"Look, this is going to sound totally weird, but can we talk sometime?" he asked me softly as he picked up his first costume. "I'm confused. I mean, girls are usually impressed by my size. But there's one who isn't. Besides you, I mean."

I smiled. "Sure, Dom. Maybe during a break at a rehearsal."

"Okay. Thanks." He winced and headed back to the dressing rooms.

I didn't bring any laundry that night. It was time to get into full investigation mode. I searched Maggie Leitner's office, not because I had any reason to suspect the acting teacher, but it would make life easier if I could eliminate her. If only I'd been able to. The ammo box filled with bullets was no big deal, given how many people carried guns on the campus. But I found a relatively full roll of strapping tape in one of her desk drawers and another in one of her file cabinets.

Now, that probably doesn't sound that odd. There are lots of perfectly innocent reasons for having two rolls of strapping tape. It can be enormously useful stuff, especially if you send a lot of packages. There was no hint that Leitner did, however, nor was she interested in stagecraft and other technical parts of theatre. She'd even laughed about how she'd flunked stagecraft when she was an undergrad. There is another use for strapping tape that I'm more familiar with, namely binding up bad guys' hands and feet to hold them so that the aboveboard Federal agents or the cops can arrest them without me or any of my fellow undercover operatives having to be around.

The fact that Leitner had two rolls of something that she didn't appear to have any use for was not conclusive evidence by any shot. If anything, it was little more than a hint that she might be something besides what she appeared to be. But it meant one more person to check out. I hurried back to the costume shop.

Sighing as I saw the light out in Kaspar's office, I debated searching it. Not because he was a suspect. After all, he was a potential victim. On the other hand, Kaspar would likely spot a search. The thing is, if a reasonably competent operative searches your home or office and you're not expecting it, you probably wouldn't notice that you'd been searched. If you're an operative and on the lookout for that kind of thing, even the best search artist's efforts are going to be noticed.

Sid and Nick met me at the costume shop right after the fast change for the ballet. The rest of the crew and I got the last of the costumes checked in, then Delia thanked us. Sid and I drove the other girls to their dorm, even though it was a tight fit. Once home, Sid made a phone call, and some minutes later, Jesse and Esther showed up.

"I installed the actual equipment yesterday," Jesse said. "We just have to activate it and connect it to your bug finders."

"Sounds good." Sid glanced back toward Mimi's house. "You said yesterday. Did she see you?"

Jesse shook his head. "I made sure she was gone before I did. Everyone else just saw a workman on a ladder. Your neighbor, though. She goes in and out at some pretty weird hours. I couldn't keep that tight a surveillance on her, but I saw her come and go sometimes during the day, sometimes at night. I was just lucky she was gone long enough for me to finish."

"Might be worth setting up a tail on her." Sid looked at me.

I shrugged. "Or I could try being more friendly. Probably wouldn't hurt your issue with the local politics."

"Glad I don't have to worry about that," Esther said with a grin. "Now, where are your bug finders?"

I'm not sure what all Esther did, but she fidgeted with my compact and Sid's and Nick's keychains. The wiring also fed into the television in the den. Esther cursed as she walked into the room.

"It's cold in here!"

Sid just looked at me. I tried not to glare back.

Nick ran outside to test the cameras, and they were, indeed, triggering an alert on the bug finders, and the VCR under the TV turned on and we could see Nick in the snow.

Sid and Jesse went back to the kitchen to make some cocoa, and I sat in the living room with Esther. Nick got sent to bed.

"We haven't had a chance to talk at all since Christmas," I said.

"Frank and I have been having a good time here." Then Esther rolled her eyes. "I wish we hadn't gone to Chicago, though."

She and Frank had left Christmas day to spend that week with Frank's family before heading to Kansas.

"I thought you liked his family."

"I love his mother. She's great. But his stupid brother, the oldest one? He's an asshole. Kept calling Frank a screw-up and asking him how he's going to raise a family directing choirs. Poor Frank couldn't say anything about the side business. His brother's not cleared for it. And it gets worse. His brother even asked Frank how he's going to handle having kids that don't look like him."

My jaw dropped. "He what?"

"Patrick's not bigoted. He's just worried that people won't accept us." Esther cursed again, both in English and Vietnamese, then sighed. "The worst of it is what it does to Frank. I'm afraid he's going to start trying to prove himself again."

"Oh, crap."

That was Frank's weak spot. Frank was a brilliant operative and really seemed to like the work. The problem was that when he felt he had to prove himself, he tended to take chances he shouldn't.

"He's already spending nights in the practice room, watching for that Kaspar guy. Hasn't seen him, but that costume place seems to be a pretty popular place for couples wanting to have sex." Okay, Esther used the really obscene term for it.

I flushed a little. "I'm not surprised. But how do they get in?"

"I'm guessing someone made a lot of copies of the key."

"That would make sense."

"Linda? Nancy?" Sid stood at the table with cups of cocoa appropriately distributed.

It didn't matter that we probably couldn't be overheard. Sid still used our cover names. We all sat down. Sid had spiked the cocoa with some of the bourbon we had in the cupboard.

"LeShawn, we've got several people for Karen to check out," Sid said. "We need to check out Carl Howard's class schedule. His wife, Raylene, was supposed to have given up some fellowship to marry him, so it would be interesting to see if that rumor checks out." He looked at me.

"We also have Terrence, or Terry, Peterson," I said. "He supposedly grew up among a bunch of White Supremacists, and they can be pretty anti-Communist. Terry says he's disavowed all that, but he is an incredibly good actor. And it's probably nothing, but we need a dossier on Maggie, or Margaret, Leitner."

"Okay, do I have permission to ask our two friends to do some of the legwork?" LeShawn asked.

"You'll have to," sighed Sid. "We can't go to Indiana or New York. But see what Karen can dig up first."

"I've got a suspect, too," Esther/Nancy said. "George Wildman. He's an engineering grad student, keeps complaining about Soviets infiltrating the U.S. My guess is that he's just neurotic but can't hurt to check."

Sid looked at Jesse/LeShawn. "Got all that?"

"Of course." Jesse did, too.

Out of all of us, he was the only one who had sought out a career in espionage, only to be turned down by the CIA. We had to believe it was because he's Black. He'd passed every test they'd thrown at him with flying colors and failed the interview. Sadly, it was only one of the reasons we referred to The Company in less than kind terms.

"We also probably have a fourth finishing student," I said. "Mark Debich. He's an acting major. Or, at least, I think he is. I got attacked the other night, and it was right off the police reports. I'd picked up Debich's coat by mistake and when he called out, the attacker ran off. Debich said he was one of the targets, that he knew why the others had been killed, but couldn't say."

"I've already talked to Randall about it," Sid said. "And he's not surprised. There may even be a couple more on campus."

Esther's eyebrows rose. "That makes sense. The really good ones would be hard to spot."

"Have you gotten anything on Steve Weber?" Jesse asked.

Sid shook his head. "Nothing yet."

"Why can't we bug his place?" Esther asked.

I winced. "We don't really have cause. Let's face it, the searches we do and all that are technically not admissible in court."

Esther was not put off. "Do we need a court case?"

"Not entirely." Sid shrugged. "Our primary objective is to find the rogue and put a stop to him. Or her. Theoretically, getting the rogue arrested and convicted would achieve that effectively. But that's not necessarily our goal. On the other hand, bugging Weber and maybe even several other folks would take an enormous amount of resources that we don't have. Monitoring the tapes from even one subject would be a full-time job for a three-person crew, and that's a lot of time to spend on possibilities, especially when we all have covers to keep intact. We may get to that point with a suspect or two, but we're not there yet."

Esther cursed again. "You're right. And I have to say, I do believe in due process."

"Okay." I smiled at her. "Why don't you give Dave our love? And tell him he doesn't need to spend so much time in the practice rooms. If he hasn't seen anything by now, decent odds he's not going to catch something."

We sent the two of them on their way and went to bed. As Sid and I usually did, we got involved in connubial bliss, and as we did, the alert went off. Once we'd finished, we both got on robes against the chill in the den and checked the VCR. Sure enough, Mimi Dearing stood outside the side of the house with her ear close to the window. She left suddenly for her place. We looked at the time on the video. It was darned closed to when Sid and I had finished. We looked at each other. It was very weird.

The next morning, I really did not want to haul my backside out of bed at five-thirty. But I did. I had the offices of several faculty members to search, not to mention the scene shop, make-up room, and Delia's office. Not that I was going to get all that searched that morning. Sid had agreed to walk Nick to the gym, then school that morning so that I could drive.

I started with the office belonging to the theatre department head, Andrew Kelleher. I didn't find anything incriminating. I will give him points. He had his porn magazines right out in the open instead of hiding them. He did not have a gun, though. I was done right before seven, which was a good thing, because the light had gone on in Dr. Dorfmann's office while I was searching Dr. Kelleher's.

I hurried to the Fitness Center and found an open treadmill. Sid and Nick showed even before I could get on and we ran together until Nick had to go get ready for school at eight.

"Find anything?" Sid asked me softly, still running.

"Not really." I gasped a little and picked up my pace. "What is it with men and pornography?"

"Have no idea." Sid glared ahead. "Something about the objectification of women is what I've heard. Which may explain why I never got off on it."

"That and you had plenty of access to the real thing is what you told me one time."

Sid chuckled, then winced. "There's a big difference between watching people have sex and pornography. There's no joy in porn, and a lot of it's downright abusive. I do not understand why guys like it, but a lot of them do."

We both got off the treadmills at the same time, but had to shower separately. I followed Sid to his office to drop off my coat and my gym clothes, told him I'd meet him at five, then reminded him that I had rehearsal that night at six-thirty. He left shortly after, and I yawned. I stayed in the Performing Arts building during my two breaks between my classes. I had a scene for directing to work on, plus another scene for my acting class. In Theatre History, we'd had a short-answer quiz on Friday on Medieval theatre. I'd gotten a B, having biffed the question, "Most Medieval artists are..." Dr. Necht told us that some smart-ass had put down "dead," which made it a true statement. However, the answer Dr. Necht had been looking for was "anonymous."

In the costume shop, the rush was on to finish the Top Girls costumes. Nonetheless, Delia told me that on nights I had rehearsal, she was okay with me leaving at four, so I didn't have to rush so much to go home and get dinner.

"Linda, you are one of the most productive people I've had working here." She sighed. "In fact, you've probably made up your hours."

"Not until next Wednesday," I said. "Unless I come in early tomorrow and Thursday again. I've only got fourteen and I need twenty."

Delia cursed and looked at her calendar. "Don't even think about coming in again until the twenty-third. Top Girls is close enough to done, and I'm really going to need you for Richard. If I need you sooner, I'll post a note on the green room door." She smiled weakly at me. "I can't keep you for more than your twenty hours. The other teachers get pissed and you are in a show."

"Okay. Thanks."

I left at four and Sid was thrilled that I no longer had costume shop hours to work around. We picked up Nick at Randall's lab, then hurried home. I dusted while Sid made dinner. We had just enough time to help clean up, then Sid drove me back to school and made a point of walking me into the building. Given that everyone knew about the week before, it made more sense that I wouldn't want to be alone.

While Dom and I were waiting for our scenes to come up, I told Tracy that we'd be just outside the director's room door, working lines. Okay, I fibbed about working lines, although Dr. Dorfmann was pushing us to get our lines memorized as soon as possible to minimize the chance of forgetting one or more. You can't really ad lib your way out of a dropped line with Shakespeare.

"So, what's going on?" I asked Dom.

He sighed heavily. "Katie Hughes. She hates me and I love her."

"Well, you did stick your tongue down her throat even after she told you not to."

"But girls like that."

"What makes you so sure?"

Dom swallowed. "They seem like they do."

"Dom, French kissing a woman is invading her space. You really don't want to do it until she invites you. If she says no, you've got to respect it. If she's playing games, you'll find out fast enough, and, really, do you want to be dating someone playing those kinds of games?"

"I guess not." He frowned. "Is it really true about the size thing?"

"Oh, yeah." I grinned, then softened. "But that doesn't mean you don't have any magic yourself. It's just not about anatomy. It's about love and commitment and treating a woman with respect and kindness."

"Huh."

I chuckled, wondering if he got it. But then I saw Raylene Howard wandering along the back hall of the building.

"What's she doing here?"

Dom turned and looked. "That's Mrs. Howard. She's on some sort of crusade against bad morals or something. She's always wandering around, looking for people necking or having sex. It's kind of creepy, if you ask me."

"Yeah, it is."

I couldn't say more, though. Tracy called Dominic into the director's room.

February 4 – 6, 1987

That Wednesday, Theatre History got canceled, so I got my stuff from Sid's office, left a note, and walked home. On a whim, I dumped my stuff inside the house, then walked over to Mimi's place and knocked on the door.

She opened it just enough for her head to peek out and looked at me, puzzled.

"Uh, hello, Linda."

"Hi, Mimi." I smiled. "Class got canceled this afternoon, and I just thought I'd ask you over for some tea, if you like."

Mimi glanced back inside. "Th... thank you. Some other time would be nice. I've got to go."

She shut the door quickly, but not before something moving in the background caught my eye. I couldn't help but wonder who else was in the house. If it were her husband, why would she hide it? I was also fairly sure he was teaching that afternoon. I thought I'd heard Esther say that she had Dr. Dearing in the afternoons, Mondays, Wednesdays, and Fridays. Nor did it make sense that Mimi would hide that Raylene was there. Or Mimi's son, for that matter.

When I got back to our house, the phone was ringing. It was Sid.

"Are you alright?" he asked.

"I'm fine. Class just got canceled, so I came home. I left you a note."

"So, you walked home alone?"

"Yeah. It's daytime."

"Honey, nobody on campus has been walking anywhere by themselves."

"Shavings." I was nettled by his tone, but he was right. And there was something else going on. "Are you alone?"

"No. You know how it is. Everybody's worried."

"Okay. Anything I can get started for dinner?"

"That sounds delicious, sweetie. No, don't call back." His tone turned a touch annoyed. "Yes, I'll be home at the usual time."

"Okay. I love you."

"Me, too."

Sid and Nick got home just after four. The menu showed chicken cutlets in chile sauce with cole slaw. Sid and I had been ecstatic when we'd found the canned sauce on the grocery store shelf. It wasn't nearly as good as the sauce our housekeeper Conchetta Ramirez made from scratch, but given that there weren't any packages of dried chiles anywhere in the store, let alone fresh chiles, we considered it a God-send. I'd gone ahead and made the cole slaw.

I sent Nick to his room to work on his homework as we had rehearsal that night.

"What was with the phone call today?" I asked Sid as he got the skillet out of the cupboard.

"Sorry about that." He squeezed his eyes shut and quickly shook his head. "What a mess. I was calling to check on you. Only Steve Weber walked into my office just as you picked up." He sighed. "I've been trying to be a little more traditionally male around those jerks in the hopes of finding something out."

"Oh. That's why I came home. I thought I'd try to get something out of Mimi."

"Did you?" Sid went back to getting the skillet on the stove and heating up some oil.

I shook my head, then got the chicken breasts out of the fridge. "I think she had someone in the house with her, but I don't think it was her husband or her son, and I don't think it was one of the other faculty wives. What about Weber?"

Sid cursed. "That's a mess and a half. His wife has been threatening to leave him since last summer and is now officially doing it. She's apparently tired of him cheating on her."

"Imagine that."

"Yeah." Sid rolled his eyes. "Imagine that." He slid the chicken breasts into the skillet and looked at me. "You know, before I gave up sleeping around, there were a lot of your attitudes about sex and fidelity that I just did not get. And even after I gave it up. I mean, I could see that me being with someone else hurt you, but I never really understood why. The weird thing is that now, I'm getting it. I knew that my values about sexual behavior weren't exactly the same as most people's. But it never really registered how different those values were. It's like you were asking the other day about men and porn, and I couldn't answer. I'm not that turned on by porn, and not at all by the whole dominatrix sadomasochism thing. I literally do not understand why handcuffs are considered a thrill. And it's not like I haven't tried any of that stuff."

I chuckled. "I don't doubt that."

"But see, for me, sex has always been about joy. I can see keeping that joy to ourselves, which is one of the many reasons I do not have the least interest in cheating on you. What makes our joy so special is that it is exclusive to us. We don't share it with anybody else, and I have absolutely no interest in doing so."

"I know, dearest." I walked over to him and ran my finger down his nose.

"Even if I did, it wouldn't mean anything more than when I do it by myself. But for Weber, and so many of these assholes, sex is about power. If they want to please a woman, it's so they have power over her. And if they cheat, it's another way of proving that they have the power over their wives to do what they want or proving that they still have the power to get another woman to submit to them." Sid shook his head. "That's why I was so curt with you today. These guys, they're so terrified of looking like their wives control them, they won't even take a phone call. The other day, Al Horton was having conniptions because his wife called him about their three-year-old, who had pneumonia. If you'd taken Nick to the doctor's and he'd gotten diagnosed with pneumonia, I'd want to know right away. But not Al. God forbid you actually call your wife to see how she's doing. I was a little worried about you being seen walking around by yourself. We do have to be careful about looking like civilians. But, hey, I missed seeing you and wanted to talk to you. How does that make you more powerful than me?"

"It doesn't." I sighed. "I don't get it, either, but I suspect it's all part of that whole messaging thing that's been making me crazy this past year. It's like you keep saying. We get to define our relationship. Not anybody else."

Sid turned the chicken breasts into the pan. "Nothing like being hoisted on one's own petard." He suddenly looked at me. "You wouldn't happen to know what a petard is, would you?"

I grimaced. "Some sort of medieval weapon? That's supposedly your bailiwick."

Sid rolled his eyes, then pulled me close to him. "I'll call Randall. In the meantime, I'm really wishing you and Nick didn't have rehearsal tonight."

"At least you'll get on top of grading papers."

He snorted, then licked the back of my neck. "I'd rather get on top of you."

"Later, dearest." I shivered with anticipation. "But back to Dr. Weber. If his wife has been threatening to leave since last summer, is it possible that pushed him over the edge?"

Sid frowned. "But how has he found out about the finishing students? The report says he has no connection with anyone in the Intelligence Community."

"Does he have any kind of relationship with Earnest Kaspar?" I got out a bottle of white wine from the fridge and opened it. We figured the wine fit with our story that we were from California.

"Why do you ask?" Sid put the cooked chicken on a plate. "Can you get me the spinach, please?"

I got the frozen spinach from the freezer and handed it to Sid. "Well, Kaspar must have some records on his students. What if Weber saw them?"

"And we can't search Kaspar's office or home because he can't know that our side is onto him." Sid opened the can of chile sauce, poured about half into the skillet, then added the spinach. "I'm going to let the chicken simmer in this a bit. Why don't you pour us a splash of that wine?"

Sid slid the chicken breasts back into the skillet and turned down the heat while I poured a small splash of wine into each of our glasses. I did have rehearsal that night and needed to stay sharp. We ate at five o'clock, got everything cleaned up, then Sid drove the three of us back to school so that Nick and I could go to rehearsal.

The next day, I again got up early, and this time searched Delia's office and found absolutely nothing that shouldn't have been there. I was glad. I liked Delia. Dr. Dorfmann had also shown up early that morning, or at least, the light in his office was on when I left at quarter 'til eight and it hadn't been when I'd gotten there at six-thirty.

Sid was just about to get on the treadmill when I got to the Fitness Center. He smiled as he saw me and gave me a nice, warm kiss. Well, we'd had a good time the night before and we were both still feeling it. As we finally pulled ourselves apart, Sid looked away and sighed.

"What?" I asked, pushing the buttons on the treadmill dashboard.

"One of the guys." Sid got on his treadmill. "He was outside and looking up at the window just now." He shook his head. "What have they got against me loving my wife?"

"I have no idea, but then I don't get most of what guys like that do or think." I started running as well. "Maybe they're just jealous that the sex isn't as good for them."

"With their attitudes? They're lucky they get any at all."

I just laughed in agreement.

Sid had to leave sooner than I did to get to his Research class. I did my weights workout, then snoozed briefly in his office since I was a little tired after the night before and having to be up so early to search Delia's office. In Acting, we were working through a variety of scenes. Fortunately, I didn't have one that day, although I was expected to take part in critiquing the work of my classmates.

But then a weird thing happened. Two of my classmates, Sheryl Withers and Andy Ferris, were doing a scene from some play that was loosely based on Othello. The end of the scene involved Andy's character strangling Sheryl's (which may be why I thought the play was based on Othello, even if it wasn't). Maggie took a variety of comments, but most of the class thought that Andy was a little flat, nor did the strangling seem that real.

"Andy," Maggie said. "They're absolutely right. Your character is not a psychopath, cut off from his emotions. He's in a rage. The other problem you guys have is that your choreography is all wrong. Here. Let me show you. Sheryl?" Sheryl walked over and Maggie put her hands on Sheryl's throat. "This is a more likely hold for a hand strangling. Now, you have to be careful, so you don't hurt anyone, but, Sheryl, your job is to make it more realistic by reacting to the grab. That means gagging and hooking into the terror you'd be feeling if someone was actually strangling you. Andy, you can't back off on the anger, either. It's a natural thing to do, but you can't be afraid of it. Now, let's try that last bit again."

I was more than a little worried that Maggie obviously knew how to strangle someone by hand. But then Andy not only touched the rage in the scene, he played it out so far that Sheryl was genuinely terrified. Maggie jumped in and literally pulled Andy away from Sheryl, fortunately, before Andy got his hands on her throat. Andy was so hooked into the rage, he fought Maggie, but she was stronger than he was.

"Okay." Maggie announced, somewhat blithely, even though she was breathing heavily. "I think that was a lesson in touching the emotion without controlling it. We'll call it done for today. Andy, Sheryl, let's talk this over. The rest of you are dismissed."

The rest of us couldn't get out of that classroom fast enough.

"That was scary," someone whimpered, added a curse word before scary.

It was. I couldn't help looking back at the classroom. Maggie had strapping tape, knew how to strangle people, and, apparently, was as strong as an ox. She might also have had access to Kaspar's office since she was a colleague. That didn't really add up to real evidence, but it was suggestive as all get out.

News of the incident was also all over the department in short order, which made Kaspar even more annoying than usual.

"She should never have let that happen," he pronounced. "As director, your job is to provide a safe space for actors to bring their darker emotions out."

"But she did," I said. "I saw her. She was right there and didn't let Andy get anywhere near his scene partner in that state."

"It is the worst sort of failure as a director when something like that happens," Kaspar continued, completely ignoring me. "The worst. I expect better of all of you. If you are going to create art, then you must speak to the basest of human emotions and realize them accurately, but you cannot endanger your other actors."

And so forth and so on.

When I told Sid about it at dinner, Sid didn't know what to make of it, either. He made the call to Red Light to see if he could get some background on Maggie since our other friend had gone to Indiana to find out what he could about Terry Peterson.

Red Light, whose real name was Scott Morgan, was one of the operatives on the courier line that Sid and I supervised when we weren't doing other things like the current undercover assignment. We had him and our friend Henry James available to do some of the out-of-town leg work that might need doing, such as checking out Terry Peterson and Maggie Leitner. Henry was also picking up the mail and phone messages from home so that we could keep our visible lives intact.

The next day was Friday. I left Voice and Diction and went over to Sid's office to eat my first sandwich of the day. Sid was there, grading quizzes.

"Wow," I said. "It's really quiet over here."

"It's Friday." Sid looked up just long enough to give me a solid kiss. "The place really clears out after one. I'd probably do a few searches except that as soon as I get ready to, someone decides to stick around."

Someone knocked on Sid's door. I slid further into the office as Sid went to the answer the knock.

"Hey, Steve."

I couldn't see Dr. Weber, but knew he was about medium height, with a round face and a couple rolls around his middle.

"Charles, you want to get lunch at the Socratic?"

"I've got my noon class, but could probably meet you there after one."

"Great. See you then."

Sid shut the door and went back to his desk. I grinned at him.

"Am I guessing we want to take advantage of an opportunity?" I said through my sandwich.

"I'll even see if I can get him to pick up the tab." Sid grinned. "Do you mind if I use the emergency card if I can't?"

I made a face. "We'll have to. It will be alright."

"Well, don't do anything unless everyone's lights are off. We don't need to take that kind of chance."

"No kidding."

I rushed out of costuming and hurried back to Humanities. Sid had been right, though. The place was utterly empty. I found Weber's office, used the passkey that I had, put my black leather gloves on, and went to work.

There was the usual porn in between the files on different classes and journal articles. Weber had filed everything by date and cross-referenced it all on a set of index cards on top of his file cabinets. The file drawer in his desk held a new rental agreement for an apartment. I wasn't sure where in Collins, but memorized the address just in case. There was also a twenty-two snub-nosed revolver and ammo for it and a bigger gun. Then I found a bail receipt from Wyandotte County courts, with an attached arrest report. Harlan Weber had been arrested in Kansas City on October 12, 1986, for causing a disturbance. The note on the arrest report mentioned that Dr. Steven Weber had been contacted shortly after midnight, then a later note, at two-twelve, a.m., mentioned that he had arrived with his father's medications.

Jesse/LeShawn had found some super tiny cameras and film to go with, and I had one in my pocket. I pulled it out and got shots of both the bail receipt (which Dr. Weber had signed on October 13) and the arrest report. Then I got a shot of the rental agreement. There really wasn't much else there.

I checked my watch. It was getting late, so I slid out of the office and almost walked right into Dr. Carl Howard. I whipped my hands behind my back to hide my gloves.

"Oh, Carl!" I gulped. "You scared me!"

He blinked at me. "Linda, what are you doing in Weber's office?"

"Is that whose this is?" I looked back at the door, then continued getting my gloves off behind my back. "Carl, the scariest thing just happened to me. I was being followed. I was in the Performing Arts building, so I ran here and hid in the first open office I could find."

"Followed? By whom?"

"I don't know. He was just really scary." I blinked as if I was trying not to cry. "And after last week... Oh, dear!"

"There, there, Linda." Carl patted my shoulder. "It's alright. I'm sure Dr. Weber won't mind. Would you like to wait for Charles in my office? I mean, I'm assuming you're waiting for Charles."

"Honey?" Sid/Charles walked up just then. "What's going on?"

"Oh, honey, it was so scary!" I fell into his arms. "I was just walking along in Performing Arts, and somebody started following me. So I ran up here and hid in the first open office I found."

"Are you sure somebody wasn't just going the same way?" Carl asked.

I sniffed. "It sure didn't look like it." I blinked again. "Maybe it was. I've just been so on edge since I was attacked last week."

"Thanks, Carl, for being so understanding," Sid said. "I'll take Linda back to my office, then get her home." Sid paused. "I thought you'd already left."

Carl sighed. "I, eh... Forgot something in my office that Raylene wants. I'll just go fetch it now."

He scurried away. Sid and I watched as he turned around and went back along the corridor to his office. As in, he didn't have any real reason to be right in front of Steve Weber's office when I'd come out. Even the men's room was down the hall in the direction of Carl's office.

Sid and I, however, continued down the hall to his office.

He chuckled. "Once again, your flair for melodrama has saved our butts."

"I sure hope so." I sighed. "Thank God, I don't have rehearsal tonight."

"Does our son?"

"We're both off until Monday, when I start again." I shook my head. "I ran into Carl face on. What was he doing heading away from his office in that direction? The parking lot's the other way. The only thing in the direction he was headed is the Journalism department."

Sid shrugged and looked down at his desk. "I have no idea and do not know how I'm going to find out beyond asking LeShawn to keep an eye out for him."

We hung around until four, with me catching up on some reading and Sid grading quizzes. Then it was time to pick Nick up from Dr. Randall's lab. I was still a little dopey from lack of sleep and Nick's chatter about his experiment washed over me. Sid let Nick and me have a little snack of crackers and cheese when we got home because there was a guest coming that evening, which meant dinner would be a little late.

Henry James is a tall man, balding, with an oddly red face. His cover was that he was Sid's father and had often acted as one, even if he wasn't. Henry rang the bell right at five-thirty. We hugged him on the porch and quickly pulled him inside. The wind had picked up and sub-zero temperatures were predicted for overnight.

All four of us automatically checked our bug finders, but nothing registered.

"Got your mail," Henry said, handing over three different manila envelopes.

"Thanks," Sid said as I took the envelopes. "It's good to see you. How are you doing?"

"Well enough." Henry had lost his wife to cancer the summer before and was still feeling the loss. He'd technically retired from the FBI, only to go right back into active duty as an undercover operative. "How are you three?"

Sid frowned. "Not getting very far, but that happens."

"So, it does."

"Can we get you any tea or water?" I asked.

Henry sank onto the living room couch. "Anything stronger?"

"We have some good bourbon," Sid said, heading into the kitchen to fetch it.

"Now, that sounds terrific."

The whole evening was terrific. Henry didn't have a lot of news for us. Terry Peterson's story had checked out.

Henry had talked to several people in Terry's hometown, including the drama teacher at the high school.

"She said he's extraordinarily talented," Henry told us as we ate warm bowls of a good chicken stew. "In fact, she wanted him to go to college in New York."

"I understand he did his undergrad degree here," I said.

"It was what he could afford on the scholarship he got," Henry said. "He's estranged from his family. His parents are in that whole Klan mentality and did not want him going to college. His teacher said that he wanted nothing to do with White supremacy and couldn't wait to get away."

"Huh," said Nick. "No wonder he's doing such a good job with Richard. He's probably been feeling like the family oddball all his life."

The conversation moved on from there to more general topics. Sid played the piano for us, as well. All-in-all, it was a nice, cozy evening.

February 8 – 12, 1987

Henry spent Saturday with us but left early Sunday morning. After mass, I called Mae from a payphone in Kansas City, then called my mother, who lives in South Lake Tahoe, just to say hi. Mama had a new puppy that she'd gotten for Christmas since her other, older dog had died the previous summer. Alas, Spot, who was some sort of Dalmatian mix, was not responding well to house training.

"And your Grandma Caulfield does nothing but complain about the snow," Mama said.

Grandma Caulfield is Mama's mother. She'd moved in with Mama and Daddy the spring before when my parents had decided to give up living part of the year near Grandma in Southern Florida. There wasn't much I could say. I simply let Mama complain for several minutes. At the same time, Sid called Stella and Sy on the next payphone over, and I had to keep Mama on the line while Stella talked to Nick so that Mama could have a chance to talk to Nick, too.

I was excited about Off Campus Office Hours. For the first time, I'd be able to stay late enough for our team meeting with the non-civilians. Both Irene and Randall were there, as was a whole collection of sweet young things from Sid's classes. Frank/David and Esther/Nancy arrived at the same time Terry Peterson did, then Jesse/LeShawn and Kathy/Karen came in. Terry made a point of sitting next to Jesse, which I thought was interesting.

Nick sat next to Randall and pulled the older man out of his customary reverie for an extended conversation about the chemistry of fermentation, of all things. Karen/Kathy sat next to me, and I asked her how she was feeling.

"Great," she replied. "The morning sickness has backed off and I think I'm starting to show."

I looked down at her waist. "Really?"

"LeShawn doesn't think so, but the pants are getting a little tight around the waist." She looked at me. "You doing okay with this?"

I'd been having a rough time when my friends got pregnant. Sid and I can't have kids of our own because Sid had gotten a vasectomy years before, and thanks to the way he had slept around so much and had picked up the odd social disease or two, the odds of getting that reversed were... Well, pretty steep. [I still somehow managed to avoid getting AIDS. - SEH]

"Yeah," I said honestly and shrugged. "I'm still working on it. Some days, the thought of having a baby utterly terrifies me and other days, it kills me that we can't." I looked around, but everyone was completely pulled into other conversations and the music coming through the restaurant's loudspeakers was loud enough to cover anything Kathy and I were saying. "As Charles says, we haven't even been married a whole year yet."

Kathy chuckled and patted my arm. "You two will work it out."

I nodded because I knew we would. I slid Karen/Kathy her envelope and the film from the search the day before so that LeShawn/Jesse could get it developed.

"Hey, Terry," called David/Frank from across the table. "You're doing Richard the Third, right?"

"Yeah, Dave."

Frank laughed. "I'm leading the music ensemble for the show. I told my historical instruments teacher that I had a class with the guy playing Richard."

"Really?" Terry guffawed. "I'll bet you really had to twist some arms to get that one."

"No. I was the first person who offered, and Dr. King said it was fine."

"Yeah, you stepped in it, Lemon." Grinning, Terry shook his head. "Don't you know that the music department hates us theatre people?"

"What? Why?"

"Mostly because we're loud and think we know everything and work for free. And we hate the music people because they think they know everything and won't lift a finger unless they're paid for it." Terry laughed.

"I was told it was just a friendly rivalry," David said.

"It is. It's just that we have to share performance spaces and that can get a little tricky at times, especially when the music people ding a set or something. Or we need live music for a show and don't have the budget."

Frank shrugged. "It's my quarter project for my historical instruments class."

"You know who else is in that show." Terry nodded at me.

"That's right!" Frank laughed. "Ms. Devereaux, you and the kid."

"Just call me Linda," I said, smiled.

"Okay." Frank shrugged. "Anyway, I met with Dr. Dorfmann on Friday."

"Yeah," said Terry. "He told us he'd set up the music people for the show that night."

Frank made a face. "I like him, but he's an odd bird. Asked me some really weird questions."

"Such as?" I asked.

"Where I came from. Why I'm getting a master's degree in music, stuff like that. Even why my wife is going for her degree at the same time." Frank shrugged. "It's like I told you guys in research. It's just a good time of life for us. We just got married. We're both at a crossroads, career-wise. We don't have any kids yet. Why not get it done?"

Frank/David glanced at me. He had just done a masterful job of passing on some vital information without calling attention to the fact that it was me that was the intended recipient.

Nancy/Esther picked up the ball. "And speaking of, if I'm going to that rehearsal with you tomorrow, we'd better get home. I've got a ton of homework."

As we said goodbye, I couldn't help grinning. Odds were better than good that she was planning on searching Dr. Dorfmann's office while he was at rehearsal. This was a very good thing since Esther is a whiz at searches. She's fast and, at the same time, meticulous. The hard part would be getting in and out of that office without someone seeing her.

The sweet young things left shortly after, then Terry got up.

"I gotta run lines," he sighed, then looked at Nick and me. "We're supposed to be off book this week."

In other words, have all our lines memorized.

Nick sniggered. "I don't have that many and I don't have to be there until Friday."

"I'll see you in costuming, Terry," I said.

I was a little nervous about that, but I'd had my lines memorized the week before. I'd only used the script to make sure I had the blocking down.

Once the civilians were gone, though, we got down to business.

"I've spotted another Company agent on campus," Randall told us. The Company was how we referred to the CIA when we weren't using ruder terms. "He's not really hanging around a lot, but he's looking for something. He's in his early- to mid-forties, about five-ten, one hundred and eighty pounds, with dark hair."

"How do you know he's with the Company?" Sid asked.

"I've seen him before." Randall shook his head. "I don't know his name, but he's been around here and there."

"Has he seen you?" I asked.

"Don't know." Randall was technically a known operative, as in the KGB knew that he was an agent. "Don't really care, either. I'm not here in any official capacity."

Irene snorted. "As if that makes any difference to them."

Randall shrugged. "It's immaterial. The reality is that we have someone looking around and I don't know who or why."

"Could he be looking for the finishing students?" I asked. "If he doesn't know about the Campus Killer, maybe he's trying to find and oust the students."

"That's a possibility," said Sid. "We'll have to make a couple more phone calls. Have we found any additional finishing students?"

Kathy shook her head. "I don't think there are any. I looked at all the students' profiles and found the science and math students all had fellowships from the Tesla Foundation. Then there was a languages student, and we have a journalism student, and their fellowships came from the Hierarchy Group. I also checked Mark Debich, and he has a fellowship from yet another organization. All those organizations are owned by Trident Scholarship Corporation. I was able to look at Trident's annual report and they fund quite a few foundations, so I could search the student records for them. Nobody else at the school has a fellowship from an organization owned by Trident, at least, not that I can see."

"Good catch," said Randall.

Karen/Kathy shrugged. "It's what I do. Oh, I also verified Dr. Carl Howard's schedule, and he does not have any evening classes."

"That's interesting." I bit my lip. "So, why would Raylene have lied about that? If she were trying to root out immoral behavior, she could have just said so."

Jesse/LeShawn grinned. "And speaking of Raylene Howard, I did a little research in the news indices." He winked at Sid. "Anyway, I found out when she married Dr. Howard. It was the usual newspaper notice, with the couple settling down here. Then did a little more digging, and she got a fellowship to study Medieval art in Germany. Based on the dates, she should have been in Germany instead of here when she got married, so I'm guessing she gave it up. Sounds to me like she has more than a little reason to be bitter."

"That may be." Sid shook his head. "But that doesn't mean she's murdering KGB agents. And how would she know who they are?"

"Carl's connection to Army Intelligence," Randall said. "We don't know how many of his old friends he's in contact with."

"And finding that out will be my job," said Sid. He frowned. "If Raylene is a medievalist, could it be she's questioning my expertise?"

"She hasn't said anything," I said. "She's catty enough that she would have at least hinted. Besides, they've been married for twenty-five years. You'd have to expect that some things would have changed in the scholarship."

Sid looked down at the table. All the pizza was gone, as was the beer.

"I'd say it's time to head out," he said. "Thanks, everyone."

We slowly got up and went our separate ways.

The next day was not a lot of fun. We had snow that night, so instead of searching Theatre Department offices, I got to help shovel. We also got a call right around seven from the school, so I agreed to meet with Ms. Westmore there shortly after eleven. Then both Sid and I looked at Nick.

"Do you have any idea what that's about?" Sid asked him.

His face went guilty. "Not really. I haven't hit anybody."

"Did you threaten to hit somebody?" I asked.

"No!" Nick gulped. "It's just that Jimmy Dearing was teasing Kristie Van Meer and standing over her and scaring her, and I just got between them and stared Jimmy down."

Sid glanced at me. "Alright. You did the right thing, but let's be careful. You knowing how to fight could be questioned and we are undercover."

"Yes, sir."

As soon as I could get out of Voice and Diction, I ran for the test school. Ms. Westmore was waiting for me and very agitated as she showed me into her office.

"You okay?" I asked, sliding into the chair in front of her desk.

"I'm fine." She sniffed and blinked back tears. "It's just that... Oh, dear. There was an incident on Friday."

"Ryan told us about it," I said. "There was a boy threatening a girl, and Ryan got in between them."

Ms. Westmore looked away. "He was perceived as a threat to the older boy." In utter frustration, Ms. Westmore slammed her hand onto the desk. "It's these asinine zero-tolerance policies! It's absolutely ridiculous that we have to write Ryan up when he was defending somebody against a bully and a kid we've had repeated trouble with. And Ryan did it non-violently."

"Please tell me you wrote up the Dearing kid. He was threatening a girl."

"Yes. For all the good it will do." Ms. Westmore shook her head. "He is the son of an eminent professor on campus." She shuddered. "I am not going to let faculty politics hold sway here. And I do have to agree with Dr. Schilling. Expelling Jimmy will only make his problems worse, not better. But the good news is, if we can't expel Jimmy, we can't expel Ryan. Only now, it's in his record. He's potentially violent."

I shrugged. "Actually, I can live with that." I smiled weakly at her. "I have to be honest. Ryan has hauled out and punched a couple kids. But each time, he was defending somebody against a bully." I sighed. "He used to get bullied a lot when he was younger, so his father finally got fed up and taught him how to defend himself. I hate the violence. I really do. But I have to say there's a part of me that's very proud that the only times my son has used his self-defense skills, it's been part of defending somebody weaker."

Ms. Westmore blinked again. "Well, there's not much else I can do. Except do some more statistical work on zero-tolerance and its effectiveness." She shrugged. "Anecdotally, I'm not seeing it. But that doesn't get very far. What we need is real data."

I smiled and got up. "I'm confident that you'll get it."

I left the office with my mind whirling. I'd heard Mimi talk about her darling Jimmy and had found out that he was almost seventeen and a good-sized kid. So, I was fairly sure Jimmy Dearing was her son. And my kid, who was three years younger and barely five-six at that point, stared him down and won? Oh, I was incredibly proud.

I was also a little worried. Mimi's son was a bully, and she was prone to standing under our window right about the time Sid and I would make love. That just did not sound like a good family situation. And if Mimi and her son were that messed up, it was always possible one or the other of them was the Campus Killer. The only question was, how did they find out about the finishing students?

Unfortunately, I had a midterm exam for Costuming that day. Okay, my grades were not likely to be that big an issue, but it was possible the case would run through another quarter, and frankly, I have my pride. I've never been a straight-A student, but I seldom got less than a B in anything, even in math.

I debated running over to Sid's office on my break between Costuming and Theatre History, but chose to focus on some schoolwork instead, and ate my sandwiches in the green room.

The one really great thing about how Dr. Dorfmann ran rehearsals was that once your scenes were run, and you'd received your notes, he'd dismiss you early. That night, Frank/David sat in the seats next to Dr. Dorfmann, who stopped us every so often to have David make a note or two. Esther/Nancy sat in the back of the room, grumbling over some homework. After I was dismissed, I said hi to Esther, then left the room.

Esther followed a few minutes later. I met her near the hall to the department offices.

"You want to do this together?" she asked.

"No." I checked for lights under the office doors and didn't see any on. "There are too many people around at night, so I'm going to hang out with my script and keep guard. If you hear me running lines, then you'll know not to come out until I say it's safe."

"Okay."

I kind of wished I could have helped Esther, but with all the people in the building and Dr. Dorfmann's tendency to come in early, we needed someone to stand guard. It was a good thing I did. I was surprised to see Earnest Kaspar's door suddenly open. The light was out in the office, so apparently, he'd been sitting in there in the dark. I bent my head over my script and read lines quickly as I paced back and forth in front of Dr. Dorfmann's office.

Kaspar glanced at me, then headed toward the other side of the building. That seemed a little odd because the door to the nearest parking lot was at the end of the hall where the offices were. I remained absorbed in my script, then knocked on Dorfmann's door.

"You're clear," I hissed.

"Not done yet," Esther hissed back.

She did finish shortly after that, though. As we started back toward the directing room, I spotted Mimi Dearing heading toward the main theatre lobby and the costume shop at the other end of the hall. I looked at Esther, whose eyes rose. I pointed her toward Mimi and indicated that I'd go the other way around.

When I came into the hall where the costume shop was, all was chaos. The Top Girls tech rehearsals continued and there was some blow up with the lighting, or maybe it was the set. As I headed toward the theater lobby, I saw Esther standing at the bottom of the stairs to the music department on the second floor and the third-floor practice rooms and costume warehouse. Esther and I started up the stairs as if we had every reason to be there, but the stairwell was almost empty. At the top, the door onto the third floor opened, and a woman giggled, followed by the low thrum of a man's voice. The door shut. Esther and I went up, listened at the door, but there was no sound on the other side.

Esther looked puzzled as we got into the third-floor hall and there were no lights on in any of the practice rooms, which all had small windows in the doors.

"I think I know where they went," I whispered and put my ear to the costume warehouse door.

The two parties in there, and I was pretty sure I knew which parties, were definitely getting it on. I pointed at the nearest practice room, and Esther used a passkey to get in. We kept the light out and I watched out the window.

"What?" Esther asked softly.

"That was Mimi Dearing we followed. And I saw Earnest Kaspar head this way while you were still searching."

"Any relationship to Dr. Dearing?"

"His wife."

Esther frowned in surprise. "He's married?"

"With a teen-age son at home. I just don't get why she'd be carrying on at this time of night. Wouldn't it be safer to do it during the day?"

"Dr. Dearing works all hours of the night and sometimes sleeps in his office." Esther rolled her eyes. "I had to get up at four-thirty in the morning three times before I was able to search his office. All I found was a handgun and porn magazines, but everybody has those."

"I know." I shuddered. "What about Dorfmann?"

"That was weird." Esther shook her head. "There is nothing in there except work-related files. Nothing personal. No guns or porn. It was as though he doesn't exist away from his office. He doesn't even have any art on his walls."

"That is weird." I saw the door to the costume warehouse open and slid back a little from the window to where I could still see, but not be seen as easily.

Sure enough, Mimi slid out, buttoning her blouse. Kaspar followed her a minute later. Mimi went down the stairs and Kaspar headed for the back stairs near the scene shop. Esther and I waited a few minutes more, then slid down the front stairs. I left Esther on the second floor and went to find Sid in his office.

Sid was pretty annoyed about Nick getting written up at the test school and decided that he would file a protest.

"I think it's more interesting about Jimmy Dearing," I told him as he drove us home. "Not to mention that Mimi is clearly having an affair with Earnest Kaspar, which possibly means that she has access to any records he may have on the finishing students."

"It does look pretty damning." Sid shrugged. "But do we have any real evidence?"

"Not really, and we have almost as much on too many other people."

"We do, indeed. What about Dorfmann?"

I told him what Esther/Nancy had said.

Sid shook his head. "He could be simply eccentric. Everything you've told me about his behavior suggests it."

"True."

Still, the next night at rehearsal, I couldn't help watching Dr. Dorfmann and wondering. Casey Limberg was having a really bad night. Her blocking had gotten changed the week before, and it wreaked havoc on her ability to get her lines right. She was in tears by the end of the night. Both of us were off the next night, but she caught me in the hall that Thursday right after Directing.

"Listen, our scene is going to be one of the last ones tonight. Do you mind running lines with me in the hall before we work it?" Her eyes filled again.

"Sure," I said, trying to smile and failing.

"Oh, no." She blinked, drawing the wrong conclusion. "You don't have to."

"It's not you." I folded my arms in front of my chest and glared back at the directing room. "It was just more nonsense from Kaspar. He went into an extended rant about how things work in Hollywood. Apparently, he'd been doing some TV work and dismissed it as completely formula. It's film that counts. It's film that's the art. He's just so full of it."

"And if you've got boobs, you're not going to do well if he can't touch them." Casey sighed. "I'm lucky I pulled a C in that class. The worst of it is, he's actually a really good director and you can learn a lot from him."

I just groaned.

As it turned out, Dr. Dorfmann wanted to run Casey's scene from the previous Tuesday before working the rest of them. Casey got through the scene pretty well, but still got permission for the two of us to go into a classroom across the hall to run lines. Casey went into the empty classroom first and turned on the lights.

Someone had seemingly gone to sleep in one of the desk/chair combos that faced the back wall.

"Who's that?" Casey went over and touched the slumped over form.

The form fell over onto the floor, long blond hair a tangle and wide-open, unseeing eyes staring up at the ceiling. Casey screamed hysterically. I held onto the contents of my stomach just long enough to spot the bruises on the throat and pull Casey out of there.

The hall filled quickly with students, with Raylene Howard on the fringes of the crowd. As Casey continued to scream, someone tried to go into the classroom.

"No! Don't!" I screamed. I looked around frantically for a trashcan, then swallowed back the lurching. "There's— She's dead. She's gotta be!"

I do not know who spotted me lurching, but suddenly there was another trashcan in my hands, and I emptied my guts into it.

February 13 - 23, 1987

I would have thought that having a dead body turn up in a classroom would mean that classes the next day would be canceled. Top Girls was still set to open that night, Friday the Thirteenth be damned, and Richard rehearsals would continue as well.

I, however, ditched classes that day. Everyone knew I had seen the body and then promptly barfed, and I just did not want to talk about it. You see, I have this little phobia of corpses, which I know is a little weird given that I'm a spy. But the first time I found a corpse was also the first time I got shot at, and I freaked, so that's what I usually do when I see a stiff. The barfing happened after I killed my first person. The one good part of the phobia is that it tends to throw people off about me.

Nick and I went to rehearsal that Friday night dressed in nice clothes. I had our knitting in my purse. Sid, also dressed up, sat in the room with us, ostensibly to help me get through after the night before. We'd already heard that the victim was Rita Kominsky, the engineering student among the remaining finishing students. From what I'd seen of the bruises on her throat, it seemed like she'd been strangled by hand. But there wasn't much time to discuss it, and as soon as Nick and I were done, we had the faculty reception for Top Girls to go to.

The faculty had been warned not to say anything about the body, as had the cast. As if that was going to keep people quiet. At least, no one really pounced on me in search of gruesome details, but that may have been because I hung tightly onto Sid's arm. We mostly chatted with some of the other cast members, and the consensus was that whoever the Campus Killer was, he had some incredible nerve. After all, as busy a place as the Performing Arts building was at night, how could somebody haul a body into a classroom there without being seen? There had been no sign of a struggle in the classroom (I had no idea how that had leaked, but it was true from what I'd seen). Therefore, Kominsky had to have been moved after she'd been killed.

The next night, we saw Top Girls. It had been a quiet day. We had a little celebration for Nick's birthday, which is also on Valentine's Day. But we'd all agreed that was one of those personal details that might get us into trouble if it got out to the wrong person. So, we pretended his birthday was coming up on some future date. Still, Sid seemed a little wistful that night after we got home from the play.

"You know, our boy is officially a teenager now," he said as we snuggled in bed.

"I know." I winced. "It's something that Mae complained about when her kids were really little. She couldn't wait for Darby to get out of diapers, and the same with the others. Then when they did, she got all weepy-eyed because they were growing up."

Sid chuckled and held me closer. "Four more years and he's legally an adult, four and a half and he'll be in college. It doesn't seem like that long at all."

"No, it doesn't."

The next day, things only got more wistful as sweet young things from Sid's classes, Terry Peterson, and all the rest of our team joined us for Office Hours at Angelo's. It started with some cutie named Darla.

"I'll bet your son was really cute as a baby." She giggled as Nick sighed.

"He was adorable," I said, grinning. I knew that for a fact, since we did have Nick's baby pictures. "You should see his first-grade picture. He was all mad about something and he would not smile for the camera."

"I had to wear that stupid gray plaid shirt," Nick grumbled.

"He's got the cutest little frown on his face." I added.

"I'll bet he did some really funny things when he was little," Darla continued.

We all smiled, but there was a light undercurrent of tension from Sid and Nick. You see, Sid and I don't know that much about what Nick was like before we met him when he turned eleven. Nick's mother hadn't even told Sid she was pregnant, let alone that he had a son. Nick has a few memories and a couple stories that his grandmother told him, but most of his infancy and young childhood are effectively lost, since both his grandmother and birth mother have died. Fortunately for our cover, I'd had a couple of stories in reserve.

"He was a handful," I said. "I remember when he was three, my cousin's baby was being christened, and at the party afterward, my cousin was changing her daughter's diaper on the couch. Ryan saw the baby naked and was utterly terrified and screamed. 'Mommy! Where's her penis? How can she go pee-pee without a penis?' And it was loud, in front of all our relatives, including my grandma, who was horrified."

Everyone at the table laughed hard and Nick had the decency to duck his head as if he were humiliated. Sid, fortunately, had heard the story before.

"Then there was the time—"

"Mom!" Nick groaned, but I could see him grinning.

"When you were four." I looked around at the rest of the group. "He spilled a whole bag of flour on the kitchen floor while I was on the phone, and then knocked over his milk on top of it, noticed that the milk beaded up on the floor, and poured out the rest of the milk trying to figure out why. He ran me ragged the whole morning, asking me why the milk acted so funny."

That also got a good laugh, and fortunately, the conversation meandered on to other topics. When the civilians had finally gone, Sid turned solemn.

"We need to get the police reports on Rita Kominsky," he said.

Frank shrugged. "I can do it. I've already cased the building and set up a reason to be in there. You want me to check the other victims, too?"

"That would be good. It would be nice to see if the cops have come up with anything else." Sid turned to Jesse. "LeShawn, have you got anything?"

Jesse slid a stack of photos onto the table. "I've got that arrest report from Dr. Weber's office that Lisa shot last week. Also, I did a little recon on that Company agent Randall told us about. Guess who he's been hanging around with?"

Sid picked up the pictures and cursed. "Dr. Weber."

"They seem to be friends. Dr. Weber told somebody that he's Noah Taplin and an old friend of his from his undergrad days."

I groaned. "The reports said that Weber doesn't have any connections to the intelligence community."

"And our people probably got that report from The Company," Sid grumbled.

Frank looked at the bail receipt and arrest report photos. "October twelve. Wasn't that the night Damian Walsh was killed?"

Sid couldn't help groaning. "So, we actually have someone with ties to the Company and a probable alibi." He looked at the photos. "I don't recall exactly what time frame they put on Walsh's death, but I suppose it is possible that Weber killed him. Just barely."

Kathy frowned. "What if there's more than one person doing the killings?"

"The handprints on the throats all seem to match, according to the reports we have," I said. "What are the odds we have two or more killers with the same size hands?"

"Really bad," said Esther. "But not impossible."

Sid rolled his eyes. "That improbable I don't think we need to deal with. Anything else?"

"Yes," said Kathy. "I noticed something about Maggie Leitner's personnel file. She got her MFA as Nadine Lipschanz. So, I picked up the report on her from Red Light, and that was her name originally. According to the report from Red Light, she checks out both as Leitner and Lipschanz. It seems she changed her name when she started acting professionally."

"Probably had an agent insist on it," I said.

"Sounds like." Sid sighed. "Alright, we can stick around a little and just chat or head out."

Irene and Randall left first, then Sid and I did, with Nick in tow.

"Mom?" Nick asked as soon as we were in the car. "Did you make up those stories about me?"

"Not entirely," I said.

Nick gaped happily. "It was one of the O'Malleys."

Mae changed her name when she married Neil O'Malley, and the kids, of course, have the same name.

"The christening story was Darby, and it was Janey's first day home from the hospital." I laughed at the memory. Darby is Mae's eldest and Janey is his sister. "He was simply horrified. Granny Caulfield had a conniption, and Mama was aghast, but Mae kept saying that the pediatrician said that they should use the correct names for body parts." I looked at the back seat. "By the way, your cousin hates that story with a passion, so you may want to use some discretion."

Nick's laugh was just a touch evil. "And Darby did the flour, too?"

"Nope. That was Ellen." I shook my head. Ellen was the next youngest of Mae's kids after Janey. "I nearly killed her."

"Was that the day I met them all?" Sid asked.

"Two days before that." I smiled at the memory. I turned back to Nick. "Your Aunt Mae was in the hospital after knee surgery, and I had to babysit for a whole week." I shuddered.

Frank was as good as his word. If anyone in the Collins Police Department noticed that an unauthorized person had come in and gotten copies made of their reports on the Campus Killer, the news never reached our ears. Sid brought home the reports on Tuesday afternoon. I was not in a good mood.

"What's the matter?" Sid asked.

"Kaspar." I groaned. "He is such an asshole!"

Sid's jaw dropped. You see, I don't swear. I just don't. I think it was because it was one of those things growing up that my mother simply did not tolerate. Even darn or shoot could get my fanny tanned when I was a little girl. I don't mind other people swearing, and Heaven knows, Sid's language often involves all seven of the words you can't say on television. On the other hand, in the theatre department, I was surrounded by people whose variations on the traditional curses verged on the poetic. Things there bit the Big Cosmic Weenie when they went wrong, and I'm not going any further.

"He is so Industry!" I paced the living room. "I mean, Kaspar goes on for twenty minutes about how Mark's scene really reflected the Truth that is Theatre, and it was a scene from Plaza Suite! Possibly one of the worst things Neil Simon has ever written. I did Moliere. The Misanthrope. I totally played into the farce. My guys were good. Kaspar just sniffs, said it was farce and moved on."

"It sounds like you achieved what you intended." Sid looked a little befuddled.

I shrieked.

"Honey, you're right." He came over and held me. "But he really is only a momentary aggravation."

"Too bad he isn't our bad guy." I snorted.

Sadly, just because somebody is a jerk doesn't mean he's the one murdering people or stealing secrets or other nefarious activity. The vast majority of the time, someone who is being a jerk is not guilty of anything worse than being a jerk.

"Anyway," Sid said. "Let's go through these reports. David dropped them off in Research today, and the least we can do is look at them."

But there wasn't anything in them we didn't already know. No one had seen anybody carting around anything big enough to be a body in the Performing Arts building the previous Thursday. The coroner's report suggested that Kominsky hadn't been dead very long when she was found, although it had to have been after six that night, because that was the last time anyone had seen her. Given that Dorfmann and Terry Peterson were in the director's room by six-thirty, it sure looked like they had solid alibis. I was kind of glad. Even so, it was a little frustrating.

"You know, Raylene was there that night," I said. "I saw her on the edge of the crowd. I was too busy barfing to question it, but she was there."

"Yeah, but is she strong enough to strangle somebody, then haul the body someplace else?"

"Admittedly, I haven't seen her, but I'm told she spends a lot of time at the Fitness Center."

Sid sighed. "We haven't ruled out Maggie Leitner, either. And you said she's pretty strong and knows how to strangle somebody."

"There is that. And there's also Mimi Dearing. Even if she did the strangling, she does have a son who's decent-sized. What if he's helping Mommy? They're not a nice pair."

"That could also account for Raylene." Sid blinked behind his glasses. "She could be doing the killing with Carl helping her hide the bodies. Or Carl could be doing it and she's just hanging around." He groaned. "This is ridiculous. There are too many suspects."

I shrugged. "So, what else is new?"

"Wait a minute. What's this?" Sid suddenly cursed a blue streak, then handed me the sheets of paper.

It was an arrest report. The arrestee was James Dearing, age seventeen, on attempted rape charges. He'd been brought in around five in the afternoon on February 12. His mother had made a statement around seven that he had only been playing games and that the victim had to have misunderstood. There was also a statement from the victim, Kristie Van Meer, that the Dearing boy had been harassing her repeatedly at school. The arresting officer wrote that he caught Dearing holding the girl down and trying to remove her pants.

My brain felt like the spinning wheels of a drag car getting ready to peel out. Sid was truly angry and paced the living room.

"And they wrote up our kid for being threatening!" he snapped. "Our son probably saved this girl from an attack. This is ridiculous."

"I know, and I agree wholeheartedly. But there's something else here that's more important."

Sid looked at me in shock. Well, there really isn't anything more important than our boy, and my blood was boiling about the school report. But there wasn't anything I could do about it at that moment, and there was one other problem.

"Honey, we also have two fewer suspects." I said. "This report has Mimi and Jimmy pretty solidly alibied for the time that Kominsky was killed."

Sid cursed again. He checked the report on Kominsky.

"You're right." He cursed. "I suppose I should be grateful. But it doesn't entirely leave them out of it if Raylene is involved."

"I know."

Sid checked his watch. Nick was due home any minute. We focused on getting dinner made and relaxing that evening since, for a change, neither of us had rehearsal. As soon as Nick was in bed, however, Sid and I went over the reports again, but couldn't make any headway. He agreed to let me talk to Ms. Westmore the next day.

In the meantime, there was little to be achieved by talking the case over and over. So, we tabled the conversation and went back to working through and sniping at each other over the budget.

"I can't wait to get home," Sid finally sighed as we got into bed that night. "You're right. We have to be careful. But can you blame me if I'm getting really, really tired of it?"

"At least, it hasn't been so cold lately."

"True." Sid nuzzled my ear. "And you are nice and warm."

"So, are you."

I really wish I hadn't said anything about the weather not being that cold. I know, offhand remarks like that have no effect on the weather, but you have to wonder about the timing sometimes. Things got downright freezing the next day. I still walked Nick over to school that morning.

Ms. Westmore not only agreed to see me, she seemed rather pleased with herself.

"I've been hearing that Jimmy Dearing was arrested last Thursday night." I glared at her as she sat behind her desk. "Apparently, he attempted to rape a girl, and I strongly suspect the girl was the one that Ryan defended a couple weeks ago."

"The Collins Police have spoken with us," Ms. Westmore said with a triumphant smile. "Shortly after that, I had a nice, long talk with Dr. Schilling."

"Oh?"

"Um, let's just say that any report that might have landed in Ryan's file has disappeared." Ms. Westmore smiled. "I probably shouldn't say this. The whole incident was a major mess on our side, too. We really try to work as a team here, and half the faculty was up in arms that a kid might get away with being threatening, even if it was in a good cause. The other half was furious that we weren't giving Ryan a medal. I mean, come on. Jimmy is four years older and quite a bit bigger than Ryan, and Ryan stood up to him, and did it non-violently. There were several of us who would have cheered if Ryan had hit Jimmy. That kid has been nothing but trouble."

"I've heard his home life is pretty difficult."

"Well, the arrest makes it easier for us to address his problems, so that's a good thing. We're just trying to work out how to deal with it on the public side of things. Jimmy clearly can't come back to school, so we're working on finding some tutors for him and finding ways to help him manage his anger. As for Ryan, I want to apologize. There was no reason to write him up. It's just sometimes tough trying to be fair all around."

"I accept your apology," I said, my voice a little grim. "Well, I'd better get going. Thanks for seeing me."

It would have been nice if I'd been told by the school what had happened, but at least Nick was out of trouble for the time being.

That night, the wind whipped up and the flurries flew. By Thursday morning, there was nine inches of snow on the sidewalks. The schools were closed, including the university. Rehearsal was canceled, too. It was a good thing. I messed my back up again, shoveling snow. It was the twisting motion that seemed to do it. At least, it wasn't that bad, and I had pills from the university health center. I still hadn't found the ones I'd brought from home.

Dr. Dorfmann called for rehearsal over the weekend. Both Nick and I had to be there on Saturday, and I was not happy with my performance at all. I wasn't sure what was wrong, but I was not happy. Sunday, there wasn't much to be gotten from the Office Hours meeting, but at least Nick and I could be there. Irene told me that Jimmy's arrest had been kept quiet. I wasn't sure if that surprised me or not.

Sid decided that the roots of my hair needed touching up and did it that evening, while I complained. The following quarter, the department was going to put on A Little Night Music, and I was required to audition.

"What are you going to do if we're done before next quarter?" Sid frowned as he dabbed the hair dye on me.

"Please, God, I hope we are." I looked up at the ceiling in fervent prayer, then shrugged. "I'll just have to leave. I'm not going to stick around even if I get Desiree Armfeldt. But all acting students are required to audition, and Jeff Necht is directing, so I won't be able to get away without auditioning. I have to come up with a song, too."

"That shouldn't be too hard. We're talking Sondheim." Sid's eyes almost lit up. "I've got it here, I think."

"You packed a Sondheim book?"

Sondheim is not easy to sing, and being mostly about the lyrics, it's not as fun for Sid to play. As soon as Sid had dried my hair so that I wouldn't stain the bed linens, he got a sheet music book off the shelf next to the piano.

"It's Broadway, in general, but there's plenty of Sondheim here." He flipped through the pages. "Here's a good one. How about Here's to the Ladies Who Lunch?"

I looked at the lyrics and laughed. "Oh, my god. It sounds like the faculty wives."

So, we worked on that, and worked on it again Monday night.

February 24 – 26, 1987

Tuesday morning, Raylene caught me at the Fitness Center. I'd searched the office of one of the Theatre professors I didn't know, Elon Boyd, earlier, and had found nothing except another gun. If I was taking my time that morning, it was because I didn't have acting until eleven.

I was finishing my weights workout when Raylene sauntered up from one of the aerobics rooms, wearing a light blue leotard, pink tights, and light blue leg warmers. She even wore a headband that matched. I got off the lat pull down machine and rolled my shoulders. My ensemble was some dark green running shorts and a slightly ratty t-shirt.

"My, that's very industrious of you," Raylene said.

I shrugged. "I don't have a lot of options. I have a bad back and the weights are the only thing that help." I smiled at her. "I hear you come by here a lot. Just aerobics or do you do weights, too?"

"Some weights, of course." Her smile was positively benign. "I agree, one must." She looked at me oddly for a minute. "You know what? We have not had much of a chance at all to get to know one another."

"I have been busy," I said.

"I think we need to go to lunch together. Why don't we?" She grabbed my arm, and, boy, did she have a solid grip.

"Well." I checked my watch. "I have class in another forty minutes or so. But I could probably go after that. Where do you want to meet?"

"How about Angelo's?" Her smile was less than sweet. "I hear you're familiar with it."

I grinned back. "That's where Charles has Off Campus Office Hours. You know, to connect with the students better."

"He's so devoted."

I smiled with pride. "He really is. Okay. I get out of class at twelve thirty. I think I can get to Angelo's about twenty minutes after that. Can you meet at one o'clock?"

"Of course I can, dear." She moved off, then turned back toward me. "Oh, and this one is on me. I know how hard it is to live on an associate's salary."

"That's very kind of you, Raylene." I smiled, but Sid was going to be hearing about this one.

Maggie let us out a little early from Acting class. I hurried to the restaurant, hoping to get the jump on Raylene, only she was already there, waiting at a table with a glass of cola in front of her. Okay, what looked like cola. It could have been a rum and cola. I didn't know how Raylene felt about drinking alcohol, but I was willing to bet she didn't approve of it. At least, on the surface, she probably didn't.

I ordered a diet cola, myself, never mind that I really hate the stuff.

"You and Charles seem to be settling in nicely," Raylene told me when the waitress had brought her a small salad and a plate of baked pasta for me.

"So far."

"And look at you, getting the big part in the Shakespeare play."

I laughed. "She's not that pivotal. But it is a nice role. It's kind of fun to be acting again. I used to in high school."

"Oh. Do you have professional aspirations that way?"

I shook my head. "Not at all. But I want to teach it. Theatre can be such a special outlet for kids who don't feel like they fit anywhere."

"Now, that's very kind of you."

"How about you, Raylene? Did you ever want to act?"

"Oh, no." Raylene's chuckle was just a touch off. "No. I only wanted to be loved by a good man and raise his children. And thank God, that is exactly what I have done."

"It must be nice to achieve a goal like that."

"I never thought of it that way, but you're right." Her smiled was just a touch tight. "It is nice. What about you?"

My smile was just a touch tight, too. "Well, we're still working on it. Thank God Ryan is a really good kid."

"I heard he was involved in some trouble at the test school."

I glared at her. "He was defending a girl who was being threatened by someone else."

"Yes, I know. Jimmy Dearing, as a matter of fact." Raylene's sigh stopped just short of sincere. "And he wasn't really threatening the girl. He's a good boy, at heart. He's just mixed up. Poor Mimi. Clarence doesn't come out of his fog long enough to recognize that he has a wife and son, let alone help."

"That's awfully sad." I focused on my pasta so that it wasn't obvious that my blood was starting to boil.

"It gets worse, unfortunately." Raylene glanced around, then leaned forward. "Poor Jimmy was arrested a couple of weeks ago. It happened off-campus, so they haven't heard about it at the test school yet."

"What were the charges?" I bit my lip.

This was the first that I'd heard about the incident apart from the police report the week before, and what Irene had told me on Sunday.

"Attempted rape. He'd supposedly been chasing one of the girls at school."

"Are you sure?" I swallowed. I was sure there was no "supposedly" about it.

"Of course! Mimi told me about it. She was so upset."

I forced a smile onto my face. "Then maybe you shouldn't be telling me about it."

Raylene shrugged. "Everyone already knows. Except the test school people. Or maybe they do, by now. It was the same day the Campus Killer struck again, so maybe not." She shuddered. "I do not know what this world is coming to. This campus used to be so safe and quiet. The whole town was a perfect place to raise kids. Now, we've got this killer. Perfectly decent boys being accused of trying to rape somebody. You know what it is. The Communists. I don't care what they say is going on in the Soviet Union these days. They've got their spies everywhere, and one of their tactics is to manipulate our media so that they seem sympathetic."

"I have heard that here and there." I nodded.

The problem was, Raylene was right to a degree. However, it was not nearly as prevalent as she seemed to think.

"In fact." She looked at me intently. "I would not be surprised if there were KGB agents on our very campus."

"What makes you think that?" I asked. "I haven't seen anybody who speaks Russian."

"Oh, they all speak English, and without accents."

I shrugged and concentrated on eating my pasta as Raylene continued in that vein for some minutes. She paid the check, although I offered to pay my share since I'd eaten a bigger lunch.

"Can I give you a lift back to school?" Raylene asked.

I checked my watch. "Thanks, but I think I'd rather walk. Clears the cobwebs, you know."

"I guess I do." She reached over and almost kissed my cheek. "It was lovely having lunch with you."

"It was. Thank you very much."

I made it to Beginning Directing just in time, and Kaspar was still late. It was a lecture day, which was great because my mind was somewhere else. Raylene had one heck of a strong grip. Whether that meant she could carry the weight of a body, that was a good question. And if she had help, who was helping her? Her husband? Mimi? Both?

I looked at Kaspar demonstrating stage pictures with the girls in class. He was having an affair with Mimi. Was she the only one? Could Raylene be having an affair with him, too? If Raylene was, could Kaspar be the one helping her? But then, why would he? The victims were all colleagues of his, people he was there to train. Even if he didn't like them, there didn't seem to be any benefit to killing them. Unless he was trying to suck up to the CIA in order to defect, in which case, having that agent, Noah Taplin, there kind of made sense.

After Directing, I went over to the costume shop. Delia was getting stressed because we only had a week and a half before Richard went into tech rehearsals, and of course, they were behind. I still had six hours to put in and managed to do three. Delia had me mass-producing tabards that would eventually have a variety of symbols on them to represent Richard, the House of York, and the House of Lancaster. They were for the dancers in the show.

I got out at six-thirty and made the huge mistake of grabbing some dinner from the Commons, and then was late to auditions, and was one of the last to do my song. Dr. Necht asked me to come back the next night to read, and I explained that we were starting run-throughs on Richard, so Dr. Necht asked me to stay a little late and read with Dominic Purslaine and a couple other guys from the Richard cast.

I was exhausted when I finally walked in the door to the house at ten-thirty. Sid and Nick were still up, and Sid was blow-drying Nick's hair.

"What's going on?" I asked.

"Time to get our roots touched up," Sid said. "I could use some help once the kid is done."

He dabbed at the base of Nick's hair with a tissue as Nick rolled his eyes. The boy was wearing his glasses and Sid had his contacts in, as usual. Sid did not want to have to get used to the lenses again.

"Well?" asked Nick.

"You're done. Good night."

They kissed each other's cheeks, then Nick kissed mine and ran off.

"What took so long?" I asked as Sid pulled on a fresh pair of plastic gloves.

"We got started late. He's behind on his English reading again."

"What are they making him read now?"

"Silas Marner."

"Bleh." Yes, I love English literature, but the Nineteenth-Century novel is not usually my preferred part of it, although Marner isn't as bad as some others.

"I agree." Sid rolled his eyes, then sighed as he looked in the mirror.

"You can barely see the roots," I said. "Why don't you leave yours until tomorrow night? Run-throughs start tomorrow, so you'll have plenty of time."

Sid sighed again, but nodded. "I'm not looking forward to you and Nick being gone every night."

"I'm off-stage a lot and there's always the costume warehouse." I began stripping for bed.

"We'll see. I have plenty of papers to grade and several offices to search." He pulled me close to him and nuzzled my ear. "And you are coming home to our bed every night."

I smiled. "That is so very nice."

I must admit, I was a little groggy Wednesday morning, and given the long day I had ahead of me, I decided not to search offices before class. Sid and I still did our hour on the treadmills in the Fitness Center, but I went and snoozed in his office before dragging my backside to Voice and Diction that morning. I did not like the way Dr. Dorfmann looked at me, though.

I did not blame him, mind you. I was not at my cheery best. Besides being tired, I was getting nervous. It felt like my performance as Elizabeth was just so much reading lines. Admittedly, it had been over ten years since I'd last done a play, so maybe I'd forgotten how it goes. But it is not at all unusual in that process for things to go flat, and I was definitely there.

I went home for dinner with Sid and Nick. We'd decided that was essential. Okay, maybe Nick wasn't so sure it was essential, but he was willing to go along with it. Then both Nick and I got our latest knitting project together. We were working on another sampler afghan, this time made of strips. Since real wool would have technically not been in our budget, we'd bought a bunch of acrylic skeins at the local Walmart. Nick and I had already completed our other sampler, and we'd sewn the squares together the week before. Nick had that afghan on his bed, although the nights were not quite as chilly as they'd been before.

Back in the directors room, the cast milled about, waiting for Dr. Dorfmann to show. Dominic Purslaine and a couple other guys approached Nick and me as we sat down near the back of the room.

"You're knitting again," Dom said.

"I like knitting," Nick said. There was a slight edge to his voice that I seldom heard from him.

"Cool." Dom grinned. He looked back at Katie Hughes, who had the other nine dancers gathered around her in the front of the small space. "I'd like to learn how to knit."

"It's a good way to absorb nervous energy," I told him.

I couldn't help grinning. Dom was clearly more interested in appearing sensitive than nervous energy. I figured it was a step in the right direction.

"Can you teach us?" Mark Debich asked, coming up.

"Sure. But it's a little hard now," I said. "I don't have any extra needles or yarn with me."

Casey flopped down next to me. "My grandma taught me how to knit when I was a kid. I haven't done it in a long time, though."

Lindsey Warburton, who was playing Queen Margaret, kneeled in one of the seats in the row in front of Nick and me.

"I've always wanted to learn how to knit," she gushed. "I don't know why."

"It's not hard," Nick said, grinning at her.

"Okay. Can you guys get over to Walmart sometime tomorrow?" I asked.

The group looked at each other and all agreed they could.

So, I wrote up a list of materials and during the break, got Dr. Dorfmann to open the department office and let me run a bunch of copies on the photocopier.

"Knitting?" he asked.

"It's good for nervous energy and once you've got the basic motions down, it makes concentrating a lot easier for some of us." I shrugged. "That's why I taught Ryan to knit. He's got attention deficit hyperactivity disorder, and it really helps keep him focused."

"I hadn't heard that." Dorfmann smiled.

"I don't know that there's any documentation on it. I just know that it seems to work."

The run through (in which we did the entire play without stopping) went on. I was still feeling a little frustrated, but when Dr. Dorfmann handed out his notes at the end of the run through, he only called me on a couple mispronunciations. At the end of the rehearsal, he looked at me again.

"You haven't found the emotions yet, have you?"

I blushed. "I thought I had."

"Tomorrow, don't think Prince of Wales. Think Ryan."

"Um. Okay."

It had been a pretty rough rehearsal for everybody. Even Tyler had messed up a few times, and it looked like his mother was going to take him to task for it. But Dorfmann spoke with her quietly as we all left.

Fortunately, it wasn't that late when I pulled the car into the garage at the house. Nick got out first and ran inside. I got the garage door down and followed wearily. Sid was waiting for us. Nick got sent to bed promptly. I stripped and headed there myself. Sid slid into bed next to me within minutes.

"Are you too tired?" he asked softly.

"Never," I said, even though I was pretty close. "I'm laying down. And to be honest, I'm not sure I can get to sleep without it, anyway."

Sid laughed. "You've spoiled me, my love. I can't sleep without it, either."

So, we made love slowly and lazily. Then I slept like the dead.

I was also able to sleep in a little the next morning. The three of us went to the Fitness Center in time for Nick to get an hour in on the treadmill, as Sid and I did. Then, after kissing Nick goodbye for the day, Sid and I did weights.

We ate dinner together that evening, and Sid made chicken tacos, one of our family favorites. Nick and I grinned because we knew why. One year before, on that day, I had officially adopted Nick. It was the first step that made us legally a real family. And please keep in mind, when I write about us becoming a real family, it wasn't about Mom, Dad, and Kid. Nick had had a real family with his first mom and grandmother. It was about Sid, Nick, and me forming a family.

It was a little hard to celebrate because I had supposedly given birth to Nick, and Sid and I had supposedly married before that. But none of us wanted to pretend the date was just like any other.

Sid decided to come with us back to school.

"I've got grading to do," he said. "Plus, I'd like to look more closely at Carl's office."

"Any reason why?"

He frowned. "I'm not sure. Just something a touch off today. He seemed like he was a little worried about me."

We got to school about half an hour early. I had another stack of photocopies, this time with drawings I'd copied from one of my favorite knitting books illustrating the two basic stitches. Almost everybody who showed up with a ball of yarn and needles got their first stitches cast on before rehearsal started. Casey and Lindsey looked at the copied instructions and got a couple rows of knit stitches in. The others had to wait until they were off stage for me to show them how to do the basic knit stitch. Nick also helped.

Rehearsal that night was really rough. Even Terry, who'd had his lines down before any of us, was blanking. I was afraid enough that the knitting was distracting everybody that I stopped showing people how between scenes. But that wasn't what was wrong. The kids who weren't knitting were in even worse shape than the kids who were.

Then came my final scene, the one where Elizabeth is bewailing the loss of her sons and confronts Richard about it. Right before I came on, I looked over at Nick and thought about how I'd feel if he'd been smothered in his sleep. It was a feeling that came all too easily. I was already worried that our side business would hurt, or worse, kill him. The tears on my cheeks were real that night. I was completely out of control, totally blew my blocking and jumbled at least half of my lines. But all I could think of was my sweet boy, his life snuffed out by an evil I faced far too often.

Nick looked worried as I staggered off the little stage. I just grabbed him and held him as tightly as I could.

"Mom...?" he asked, with that frightened tone he so often had any time his father and I had to do something dangerous.

"I'm alright, honey." I said, gasped. "It's okay."

I got the first note that night. Dr. Dorfmann just smiled at me.

"You touched it, didn't you?"

"Yeah," I said, still feeling shaky.

"Good. Remember what you felt and control it."

"Okay."

Actually, there weren't that many other notes.

"That should do it for tonight," Dr. Dorfmann said. He looked us all over. "You all have been working very hard. I know tonight seemed very rocky, and it was. But this is a good thing. And the reward for all your hard work is a few nights off. I do not want any of you thinking about the play until Monday night. Do not run lines. Do not look at your scripts. Do not think about Richard. Monday night, refreshed and renewed, we will once more into the fray. You are dismissed."

February 27 – March 7, 1987

Sid was thrilled to hear that we had a few days off. Friday morning, after telling me he hadn't found anything in Carl's office, he made several phone calls. Better yet, I discovered that Theatre History was canceled that day. Apparently, Dr. Necht was exhausted by casting the musical. However, the cast list was up first thing in the morning. I sighed in relief that my name was not on it.

Sid and I picked up Nick from school at two-thirty.

"What about Lab Rats?" he asked as we got into the car.

"I've already talked to Dr. Randall about it," Sid said.

We grinned at each other.

"Hey, why aren't we going home?" Nick asked.

"We're going to visit my dad this weekend," said Sid.

Nick looked puzzled. "Henry? Why can't he come here?"

"That's just what we've told everybody," I said, smiled. "We'll actually be taking a flight out of here for a couple days."

I have to say, that weekend was exactly what we needed. We ended up in New York. I felt a little guilty that we didn't contact Sy Flournoy, Stella's lover who split his time between Los Angeles and Stella, and New York, where he was the head of the strings department at Julliard. But not that guilty.

Sid got us a suite at the Park Plaza Hotel. Nick saw the TV and the labels on it and crowed.

"We've got cable!"

We had decided that we wouldn't get cable in Kansas because even Nick doesn't watch that much television. But the siren call of MTV entranced Nick that evening, so we indulged in room service and stayed in.

Sid and I sat in another part of the living room area and snuggled. He smiled at his son.

"Family time, right?" I asked.

"Yeah. I've been trying to figure out how we should celebrate our anniversary." Sid smiled at me. The one-year anniversary of our wedding was that Sunday. "The funny thing is, while the wedding thing is supposed to be about the two of us, it's always been about the three of us as a family."

"It is." I laid my head on his shoulder.

Sid softened his voice so Nick wouldn't hear. "You seem a lot happier lately."

I had been having a hard time coming to terms with being a married woman. Then there was the whole not being able to get pregnant thing.

I shrugged. "I'm doing what I do. Searching offices, weaseling out answers without letting on why I'm asking."

"Still..." Sid squeezed me, then let out his breath. "Even Kathy's pregnancy hasn't thrown you off."

I made a face. "I don't know why, but you're right." I looked at him. "Sid, do you want another kid?"

"Um. Not really." He frowned. "But at the same time, I didn't want the one I have, and that's working out really well. I didn't want to get married, either, and yet here I am, very happily married. So, I don't know." He smiled softly. "A little girl would be nice."

I chuckled. "She'd be so beautiful, with your dark, wavy hair, your chin dimple, and those gorgeous blue eyes."

"As long as they're as big and round as yours." Sid sighed. "I suppose we could try to find a sperm donor with the right traits."

I rolled my eyes. "There is no point in doing that." I shrugged. "The thing is, I don't want a baby. I want *your* baby. The fruit of our love. And since that isn't going to happen, that's what I deal with."

"What do you mean?"

"Well, there will always be that bit of sadness that we can't have children together. On the other hand, we're not dealing with two a.m. feedings, diapers, toddlerhood. You know how much I love Mae's kids, but I've said it before. It's a heck of a lot more fun being an aunt than mommy. The kids get cranky, Mae and Neil get them. They start squabbling, Mae and Neil get to sort it out. We get to be the indulgent aunt and uncle and only rarely have to be the authority figures." I shook my head. "Your kid would be special, but it's your kid that counts. And I have that and he's a wonderful kid. If I can't have one of yours, myself, well, I knew that going in." I shrugged. "Having you is more than worth the occasional pang because I can't have your baby."

"Still, if it would make you happy, I could check with the doctors again."

"No! It would be major surgery that would probably not work, and even if it does, who's to say I won't have the same problems carrying a baby to term that my mother did? So, unless you are really pining to be a daddy again, I don't think it would be worth it."

"You're not just saying that because you think that's what I want to hear?" Sid's gaze was just a touch worried, and I'm afraid he'd had cause over the previous year.

I thought. "Don't think so." I looked over at Nick, who was singing along to Nothing's Gonna Stop Us by Starship. I couldn't help thinking about my meltdown at rehearsal the night before. "Nick is definitely enough for me. He's more than enough. In a lot of ways, I feel so incredibly lucky to have him."

Sid nuzzled my ear. "So do I. I'm incredibly lucky to have both of you."

The next morning, we went to breakfast in the hotel's tearoom. Nick remembered that the wedding anniversary was the next day.

"Do you guys want to take some time off and be by yourselves, or something?" he asked.

"That's so sweet of you, Nick." I grinned. "Or do you have an ulterior motive?"

He laughed. "Not really." He made a face. "It's when you and Dad were talking last night, and Dad said the wedding was about the three of us. I don't know what you guys talked about after that. But I couldn't help thinking, you were right, Dad. Those four days last year were about us becoming a family. I know we keep talking about that, but you know, it's important."

Sid laughed. "Aren't you supposed to be establishing an identity apart from us?"

"Huh?"

AMATEUR THEATRICALS

I smiled. "It's what being an adolescent is all about. Learning who you are as a person apart from your parents."

Nick shrugged. "I know who I am. But this family thing. We're still new at it. And it has been really cool. Can we have the adoption and wedding anniversaries as our family time? Not just this year, but all the time?"

"I think that's a terrific idea, son." Sid smiled.

Funny thing is, I think both our eyes were filling.

To Breanna, 2/22/01
Today's Topic: The Family Weekend
So, that's how The Family Weekend started. I felt really proud when Dad said it was a good idea. He and Mom were always good that way. I had no idea then how rare that was. I thought just my first mom and grandma had a problem.

I know most folks celebrate their wedding anniversaries as a couple, but like I told you, my parents' wedding was just as much a part of making us a family as Mom adopting me.

The important part is that you are part of us, too, and that happened before we decided to get married. It's how I know we're doing the right thing.

It was a truly lovely weekend. We saw a show on Broadway, slept in on Sunday, and got room service for breakfast. Then we had to go back to Kansas. We got in at about eight that night and were quite pleased to discover that it hadn't snowed while we were gone.

Monday, I went in on my second break to get my Richard costume fitted, which was kind of exciting. After Theatre History, I got my last three shop hours in. I had just enough time to get home for dinner, then Sid brought Nick and me back to school for rehearsal.

Tuesday afternoon, after Directing, Mark talked me into going over to the Commons to eat. Well, I wasn't going to eat, although I had enough change for a bag of chips and decided I'd get one. As we walked over, I got the sensation of being followed. Sure enough, Earnest Kaspar seemed to be coming our way. While Mark and I sat down and he ate lunch, I caught another glimpse of Kaspar. He wasn't headed for the Socratic. He also came back into the Performing Arts Building right after Mark and I got back there. I had to leave Mark in the Green Room to get Nick from Lab Rats and us home for dinner.

The next day was Ash Wednesday, and Sid rousted Nick and me out early so that we could go to church and get our ashes before we went to school.

"I don't know why," I grumbled as he drove. "It's not like Ash Wednesday is a holy day of obligation."

"A what?" Sid glanced at me.

"Holy day of obligation, where you have to go to mass as if it were a Sunday. Ash Wednesday isn't one of them. Immaculate Conception, Assumption of Mary, All Saints, those are still on. Ash Wednesday never was."

Sid shook his head. "How the hell do you keep track? Anyway, it's all about our cover. Al Horton asked me yesterday if he'd see us at Mass."

So, Nick and I got our ashes on our foreheads. Sid could have, but since it was established that he wasn't Catholic, he decided not to. Al Horton was not at the service.

Later that afternoon, as I got out of Theatre History, I saw Mark and Terry heading over to the library. Kaspar wasn't right behind them but was definitely following. So,

I decided to loosely tail Kaspar. Once Mark and Terry disappeared into the bookshelves, Kaspar sped up and started checking aisle after aisle. I slid behind yet another shelf and kept a close eye on Kaspar.

"Interesting that you're keeping such a close eye on your friend, there," said a voice behind me.

I yelped and jumped. The man behind me was about five-ten, dark-haired and reasonably slight. I shrugged.

"It's some other friends of mine." I gave the man a weak grin. "He's been following them."

"And you spotted him tailing you yesterday." The man laughed. "I'd heard there were some Fifty-Three-Q folks hanging around."

Fifty-Three-Q is the official name for Operation Quickline.

I looked over at where Kaspar was still trying to find Mark and Terry.

"Who are you?" I demanded softly.

"Call me Noah Taplin." The man chuckled. "I'm in Division One."

Division One meant that he was with the main part of the CIA, rather than one of the shadow agencies.

"Why are you here?"

He nodded at Kaspar. "Same thing as you. Trying to figure out if there's a rogue agent we need to take care of."

"You're thinking Kaspar?"

"Not really." Taplin looked at me. "You got something on him?"

"No. It's just that he's been acting a little hinky."

"Why would he be killing the moles? They're on the same side."

I shrugged. "If he's trying to defect and wants to make a peace offering to your crew."

"He's not defecting. Besides, even if there was some competitive BS going on, he'd have to know his bosses would have him taken out pronto."

"True. But why is he following that kid?"

Taplin frowned. "He's probably trying to protect him. Good old Fedor is that kind of guy."

I looked over at Taplin. "You know him?"

"Just from observation. They inserted him into the Hollywood crowd about ten, fifteen years ago. It was a perfect post from their perspective. A chance to manipulate our media, plus access to all those defense plants out there. Then, about six years ago, he's getting some plum TV gigs, and they decide to promote him. They pulled him out and sent him here to teach baby moles how to fit in. Finishing school is considered a good gig, you know. Not much work. Nobody shooting at you. And Fedor's students do really well when they get into the field. Or they would if we didn't already know about them. I can't imagine him taking too kindly to someone taking out his kids."

"I can't imagine that, either." I went back to watching Kaspar. "So, how do you know Steve Weber?"

I smiled as his eyes opened a little wider. He hadn't expected me to know that.

He played cool with a shrug. "Just like he said. Old college friends. I'm using that as my cover to see what's going on here."

"What are you going to do if Weber is the Campus Killer?"

AMATEUR THEATRICALS

Taplin snorted. "He has no way of knowing who the moles are. Plus, I know for a fact that he's alibied for Agnotti. He was visiting me in Wichita those three days. His wife had kicked him out again."

I didn't quite curse but wanted to. "Well, thanks for the intel. Do you want a way to get ours?"

"Why?" Taplin laughed and sauntered off.

After checking my watch, I decided to get a couple of extra books. I did have a term paper to write by the day Richard would open. I also stopped by the department office to ask about a couple classes for the next quarter, since it was time to register for that. As I waited for Dr. Kelleher, I noticed the department scrap book. The secretary said it was okay to look at, so I thumbed through the pages. Each play had a small copy of the play's poster, a cast list, dates, who directed, reviews, and so forth. One caught my eye and I sighed.

Frank/David was at rehearsal that night. He'd already taught the dancers a couple of Gregorian chants and alternated between guitar and recorder to demonstrate where the music would go and what it would sound like. After the rehearsal, he hurried out while Nick and I gathered our knitting. Dom, Casey, and Lyndsey held us back to ask about how to do a cable stitch. I showed them briefly, then said I could show them again the next day between Acting class and Directing.

Nick and I went upstairs to the bridge to the Humanities building. Frank and Esther were there in Sid's office, and Esther was not in a good mood.

"Wildman is alibied for Kominsky," she said. "He works at Walmart every night except Monday and Wednesday. I found the work schedule for the week Kominsky was killed. He clocked in by six and clocked out at eleven, and he was assigned to a register that night. If he'd left, it would have shown in the paperwork."

Sid shrugged. "Well, that narrows things down a bit."

"We're going to narrow them a little more," I said, flopping onto the office couch.

I told them what Taplin had said.

"Annoying," Sid said. "But expected. Weber is also alibied for Walsh, and we figured Kaspar was unlikely, anyway."

"Plus, there's what I found this afternoon. Maggie Leitner directed Our Town last November and Mark Debich played the Stage Manager. The show opened on November fourteen, which means they were in tech rehearsals on November ten."

"The night Agnotti was killed," Frank groaned. "We don't have anybody left."

"Couldn't Debich have snuck out between scenes?" Esther asked.

"The Stage Manager is on stage the entire play," I said. "And according to one of the reviews, the entire cast was in this production. So no sneaking out."

"We have the Howards." Sid shook his head. "I haven't been able to find anything on Carl's military history, but Henry said he should be able to get us something on that. David, Nancy, why don't you meet with me tomorrow after Research, and we'll get LeShawn in on this, too. I think it's time to install a bug or two."

By Thursday night, the show was running well. That promptly fell apart on Friday night, with the start of technical rehearsals. Nick was amused by the idea of wearing makeup and told me he did his with one of the makeup crew assisting. I was supervised while I did mine, but the crew person was impressed, as was the crew head. We got our costumes and were each given a locker. I forgot to take my wedding rings off.

We ended up starting late and ran even later. I set up my wireless transmitter in the dressing room, where it could pick up what was going on, slipped out of my costume during my first break, then called Sid and we met in the Costume Warehouse. Fortunately, there were no interruptions, and we both felt a lot better afterward. The rehearsal, itself, ran forever. It was after midnight when we got home.

Which did not make things any easier that next morning. We overslept. Nick and I scrambled to get chores done while Sid roasted a whole chicken. As the bird cooked, he finished his chores. We all set the table, then I made a salad while Sid worked on getting some green beans ready to be cooked, and mashed potatoes. Once the bird was out of the oven, Sid made gravy, something he usually does only on holidays.

We had guests coming. Sid had talked Carl into bringing Raylene over for lunch that day. After all, it was time we entertained them. They showed up right on time at twelve-thirty. I was wearing my transmitter and earpiece, so as I took their coats to the bedroom, I signaled Jesse and Esther.

The next trick would be making it look like I'd done the cooking and not Sid, one of the reasons we'd made sure everything was ready before Carl and Raylene arrived.

"Can I get you anything to drink?" Sid asked as I came back into the living room. "We have water, tea."

"Got anything stronger?" Carl asked from the couch.

"Will bourbon do?" Sid already knew that bourbon would.

"Sounds nice, with a little bit of water."

Sid smiled. "Raylene, what can I get you?"

"Oh, honey, I don't drink spirits." Raylene smiled as well. She sat next to Carl.

"Do you drink wine?"

"Well, a little white zinfandel every now and again."

"We just happen to have a bottle." Sid headed to the kitchen to get the drinks prepared.

He also had a couple bottles of passable chardonnay, and poured me a glass of that, as well. Nick had come out and said hello to the guests, then went back to the den to read or watch TV until time to eat.

I brought out a plate of cheese and crackers and placed it in front of the Howards.

"It's so nice to see you folks settled in," Raylene said, taking a cracker, but not any cheese. "I hope you're managing with all our horrible weather."

"It hasn't been too bad," I said. "I did my undergrad degree in Wisconsin and met Charles there, as a matter of fact."

"Are you originally from Wisconsin?" Carl asked.

"No. We were both raised in California. Charles had just gotten his music degree and was touring with a band when they went broke in Madison. Charles found a job doing instrument repair and liked being there, and we met through friends."

"How nice." Raylene's smile got a little tight. "When did Charles start studying history?"

"He actually started school for that when Ryan started kindergarten." I smiled.

"Raylene, Carl, don't you have kids?" Sid asked, bringing in the drinks on a tray.

"Three," said Carl. "They're all grown now."

"Any grandkids?" He handed out glasses, then sat in one of the easy chairs.

Raylene shifted. "I'm afraid not. But we keep hoping there will be soon. Tell me, Charles, when did you get that Cavendish Fellowship?"

"My second year of PhD course work. I was getting to the point where I needed to do some research in England, and it really helped."

"I'm afraid I'm not familiar with it," Raylene sipped her wine.

"Raylene," Carl growled.

"It was actually a fairly new one," Sid smiled and sipped from a glass of bourbon along with Carl. "That's one of the reasons I went after it. Not as many applicants. And it was also strictly for Loyola Marymount candidates."

I checked my watch. "You know, I think we should go ahead and serve lunch now. The chicken's in the oven and I don't want it drying out."

"I think that's a great idea, sweetheart." Sid got up. "I'll go get Ryan."

Sid took over carving the bird at the table. I put out the gravy in a gravy boat, then put out bowls filled with salad, green beans, and mashed potatoes. It was all delicious and even Raylene couldn't find something to comment on.

"You are quite the cook, Linda," she said, her smiled getting tight again. "I don't know how you manage to feed these strapping men of yours and still find time to go to school and be in a play."

I smiled back. "It's simply a matter of being organized."

"Linda's an amazing woman," Sid said, smiled fondly at me.

We both caught the quick glare Raylene shot Carl.

"You're so lucky, dear," Raylene said, then looked at me. "You're a teacher, you said?"

"Yeah. High school English."

"Where?"

"Marshall High, in Los Angeles."

"Raylene," Carl growled again. He smiled at us, then glared at his wife. "I'm afraid I must apologize for my wife's nosiness."

Raylene's bottom lip quivered.

"Um, Mom, Dad, can I finish my lunch in the den, please?" Nick put in quickly.

I kept my eyes on Raylene. "I think that would be an excellent idea, son."

Nick grabbed his plate and silverware and vanished.

Raylene sniffed. "We discussed this, Carl."

"You discussed this." Carl suddenly looked at Sid and me. "Again, I apologize."

"It's alright," I said. "Charles and I fight like cats and dogs all the time."

"Well, we will not offend you with our disagreements," Raylene snapped, throwing her napkin onto the table. "If you will excuse me. I think I need to go home just now."

"Little Red, don't let her!" Esther's voice rang in my ear.

Raylene stormed out of the house. I grabbed her coat and ran after her.

"Raylene!" I yelped.

At least she stopped walking toward her house. Snow flurries filled the air.

"Here's your coat," I said softly.

"I am sorry about that."

I shrugged. "It's okay. Men are like that."

Well, Sid wasn't. Come to think of it, my father wasn't, nor was my brother-in-law.

Raylene blinked back tears. "I have given my entire life to that man."

"You obviously love him."

She took the coat from my hands. "And he loves me."

"I know."

"Do you?" Her eyes pierced mine. "I gave up a prestigious fellowship for him."

"So, I've heard."

She looked down at her feet. "I didn't want it. I only applied because I thought Carl didn't want me. Only when I got it, he came running. We've been together ever since. It was everything I wanted." She shook her head, then looked at me. "I was snubbed and harassed by a lot of the women PhD candidates and faculty because I gave up that fellowship. They thought it was a tremendous failing on my part. Not a failing. A betrayal. That's what hurt the worst. I just wanted to be a good wife and mother, and they thought that wasn't good enough."

"I'm so sorry." And I really was.

"I have done my best to be what that man needs. Maybe I shouldn't have been so nosy about you two today, but you're so different."

"We do come from California."

She laughed bitterly. "That would account for a lot of it. But the way the KGB is infiltrating our country, I have to wonder about you two."

I suddenly laughed. I couldn't help it. "I'm sorry. I don't mean to laugh. But you think we're KGB agents?"

She stiffened. "That does sound a little ridiculous now that you say it."

"No." I put my hand on her arm, still gasped and trying to contain my laughter. "I can see where you might wonder that. I really do. We're just not. We're anything but." I took a deep breath and had a sudden inspiration. "But... You're not the first person to think so."

"I'm not?"

"We're not. Honestly. I get that Charles' fellowship seems a little weird, but it isn't. The problem is..." I looked around the street. "Can you keep a secret?"

"Of course."

I didn't believe that, but didn't care. "Charles' mother was a Communist. She was an American Communist, but she was part of the party in the Fifties."

Okay, Sid's mother is technically his aunt Stella, and I don't know if she was a formal member of the party. But she did espouse those beliefs until the early Seventies.

Raylene's jaw dropped.

"The funny thing is," I continued. "Charles wants nothing to do with any of that. In fact, he's really embarrassed by his mom. That's why I'd really appreciate it if you didn't say anything."

"We're clear," said Jesse's voice in my ear.

"Do you want to come back and finish lunch?" I asked Raylene.

She smiled and agreed. We crunched through the newly fallen snow back to the house. Carl seemed pleased when we walked into the living room. Sid made a point of warming up our food in the microwave, and we had a pleasant time until Nick and I had to hurry back to school for rehearsal.

Carl had told Sid what Raylene had been thinking about us. We both agreed it was pretty funny and ironic as all get out.

March 9 – 13, 1987

I do not understand how or why, but it seemed like the knitting got really out of hand over the weekend. Suddenly, half to two-thirds of the cast and crew were knitting, and the rest were complaining about the balls of yarn and needles left all over the place. I tried to emphasize that people should keep their projects under control, but that was not entirely heard.

Part of the problem was that except for Terry, almost everyone in the cast had some significant off-stage time, and for some reason, most of us waited in the theater's house (aka the audience seats) until our scenes came up.

I have to say, part of that may have been the news that burned through the entire Theatre Department Monday afternoon. The Campus Killer had struck again. Student Greg Grimbacher was found dead next to the library. The weather had warmed up a little and the snow that had fallen on Saturday had melted just enough to reveal his body. The scuttlebutt was that Grimbacher had been killed on Saturday because that was the last time anybody had seen him and the last time there'd been any snowfall.

I ran to Sid's office between Costuming and Theatre History.

"Yeah, I've heard what happened," he said the second he saw me.

"It also means the Howards are alibied. They were with us from the last time anybody saw Grimbacher until after the snow started falling."

"Which I am also aware of." Sid glared at me, then softened. "I'm sorry. I don't mean to be so cranky. But you do realize that all of our best suspects are now alibied and out of it."

I sighed. "I know. They're not all entirely out of it."

Sid just shook his head. "So, what do we do next?"

"I have no idea." I blinked. "There's got to be a way to break this."

"We'll find it." He sighed profoundly. "I have no idea how, but we will. In the meantime, we live our lives as the Devereauxs."

Poor Sid. I must admit, Nick and I were having a lot of fun with our covers. Nick loved his school and doing chemistry experiments with Randall. He loved being part of the play. I certainly loved being part of the play and was enjoying most of my coursework. Sid didn't mind teaching history and research techniques, or even grading papers. It was his colleagues that made him crazy.

Monday night, the slightly warmer weather gave way to a nasty cold snap that resulted in an ice storm. Tuesday morning, Nick was entranced by how the leafless bushes in front of our house were encased in clear ice. It was gorgeous, but dangerous, as Nick promptly found out when he tried running down the driveway and landed on his backside, thanks to the ice. I made a point of spreading salt on the driveway and the walk.

Sid was still in a grumpy mood but drove us to rehearsal and worked in his office that night, writing up the final exams for his classes.

"Honey," he asked as we cuddled before going to sleep. "Please tell me I never saw you as merely the gratification of my carnal desires."

"What?" I laughed.

The tech rehearsal had gone okay. There had been a couple problems with the lighting, but we'd gotten out before eleven. Sid had driven Nick and me home.

"Al Horton and Bob Westin." Sid sighed deeply. "Sometimes even Carl, by the way. All they do is run their wives down, then complain that they don't get enough sex. I know I was focused on a woman's desirability at one time. But I don't think I saw women as solely the means to my gratification."

"No, I don't think you did." I kissed his cheek. "I remember us having a conversation where I thought that being good in bed as one's primary quality wasn't a lot, but you thought it was a great deal. Still, I never saw you treating any of your girlfriends like objects. I mean, the sex may have been all there was to the relationship, but that was on an equal basis."

He winced. "But my whole justification for my lifestyle was that I was not hurting anybody. I didn't see women as objects. Yeah, it was all about the sex, but it was a mutual thing."

"I know, lover." I smiled at him. "You were the first real threat to my honor that I had ever known. If it had been about me as an object for your gratification, I would have seen right through that, and we would never have had our relationship."

"You're not just saying that."

"No way. Yeah, I get that these guys are idiots. I think the reason that you're having so much trouble with them is that you don't think like they do and never have. And yet, you got awfully close to that kind of thinking."

He squeezed me. "You're probably right. And if I did, I hope like hell that I have gotten past it."

"I wouldn't be here now if you hadn't."

He reached over and kissed me. "You are a gem. And if I ever forget that, you have my permission to kick me where it hurts."

"I'm just me, sweetheart. But, yeah, I'll be happy to remind you that you seem to like that."

He chuckled. "You know, I think I'm finally getting to understand why you don't see yourself as the sensual woman you are. If it's normal for guys to see women like those other asses do, then, yeah, I wouldn't want to see myself that way, either."

"I'm just glad that you see me that way." I nuzzled his ear.

He kissed me with the kind of warmth that usually led to lovemaking, but we'd already done that. He chuckled and we cuddled and fell asleep.

Wednesday, I ditched classes so that I could write my term paper for Theatre History, which was due that Friday. I wasn't going to be able to write it in the evenings, and Sid had agreed to read it over for me. I went ahead and typed it but was pulling my hair out by the time Sid got home just after four.

"What's the matter?" he asked.

"I keep making mistakes and I can't correct them," I groaned. "I've been using the word processor on the computer for so long, my regular typing is a mess! Thank God, this is the last page."

"You were going to have to re-type it, anyway, weren't you?"

"I know. I'm just used to fixing it as I type. I'll have to ditch class tomorrow to get it re-typed."

"We'll see." Sid picked up what I had typed so far.

"There. Done." I pulled the sheet from the typewriter. "Do you want me to help with dinner?"

"I'm just making spaghetti with artichoke sauce." He stopped reading long enough to make a note.

"At least, I don't have to put the footnotes in the body of the paper. He said we can put them on a page in the back."

Sid sent me a mock glare. "When you taught that class, you wanted the footnotes in the body."

"So, you'd learn how to do it." I grinned and got the dusting rag. "Just because I know how to doesn't mean I want to."

"Whatever."

Sid drove us to school again for rehearsal, then went to his office there. Things were settling down with the show, although almost all the cast was still spending their off-stage time in the house.

"Where is it?" Dominic hissed while Richard was getting ready to take out Buckingham.

"Where's what?" Casey hissed back.

"I'm missing a ball of yarn and a needle. I thought it was back here."

"You might want to wait until they bring the house lights back up."

Dr. Dorfmann shot us all a glare, then went back to making notes.

"This is wrong!" boomed a voice from the back of the house.

We all looked, our jaws hanging open.

Kaspar stood just under the control booth's window. "It's all wrong!"

He whipped around and left the theater, his stride just a hair off steady.

"Well," said Dr. Dorfmann. "I guess that's what happens when you spend too much time alone in an office with the lights off. Let's continue."

We did, but no one was happy about it. Terry was furious. At the end of the rehearsal, Dr. Dorfmann staged the curtain call and ran us through it a couple times.

"Now, let's do our notes and then you people can get out of your costumes." Dr. Dorfmann went to the foot of the stage and looked at all of us in the house. "I think the first thing I want to say is that there will always be critics. I won't say the critique we got tonight was particularly helpful, but it won't be the last time any of us get that kind of comment. I have faith in what we're doing here, and I have faith in all of you. Each and every one of you has added to my vision in wonderful, amazing ways, ways that I couldn't have imagined. I have always loved this play and I love what everyone here is doing to bring it to life. Each and every one of you, from the stage crew to the lighting crew to the dancers, our musicians, and our actors. Now, do we need to fix things? Massage them along? Of course. We can always be better. But you are already good. Now, Terry, I like the twist on the opening monologue, but maybe you can take it a little further."

Dr. Dorfmann went through the notes at a normal clip. How he was able to take Kaspar's comment in stride, I have no idea, but he was a marvelous example to the rest of us.

"Clear out quickly, please," Dr. Dorfmann said as he wound up. "And tomorrow night, everyone stays backstage. I do not want to see anyone in the house."

Good example or not, everyone was still furious with Kaspar. I got out of my lovely white Medieval dress with red fox fake-fur trim and coned headdress and took it all back to the costume shop before washing my face. When I came out of the dressing room, Dom, Terry, and Nick were standing in the hallway talking. They saw me and Nick shot me a guilty grin.

"What are you three up to?" I snarled.

"We were just thinking about a prank," said Nick. "Nothing big."

I glared at Dom and Terry. "I'm counting on you gentlemen to be mature, good examples for this young man." Then I turned on Nick. "And you know better."

Nick rolled his eyes and heaved a sigh laden with adolescent angst.

"I'm sorry," said Terry, liberally added curses to his comments. "I'm still pissed. It's bad enough that something like that is way unprofessional, but to do it to Dr. Dorfmann. Dorfmann is the kindest, most loving person in this department. Never has a bad word to say about anybody. When he critiques you, he's really good about making you feel okay in spite of it. He's been there for me plenty of times since I got here, and I'm not the only one."

Mark Debich walked up. "He's been there for me, too. I don't know how I would have gotten this far without

Dr. Dorfmann. Kaspar likes to think he's helping, but he's such an asshole."

"And it's not like Dorfmann has had an easy time of it," Terry continued. "Have any of you guys been in his office? It's, like, bare. His apartment is the same way. I asked him why once, and he said that he had a wife years ago, and she died giving birth to their stillborn baby. He's still grieving for her. Is that the saddest thing you have ever heard or what?"

"It is sad," I said. "I'm so glad you care for him."

I put my hand on his left shoulder and he suddenly winced and pulled away.

"I'm sorry," he said with a slight smile. "The dermatologist found something funny there and cut it out."

"Ow." I said, but I couldn't help grinning.

Terry grinned back.

"Well," I said. "Ryan and I need to get to his father's office. Do you three guys need a ride anywhere?"

"No," said Mark. "I've got my car."

"Well, stay together, please. It will be safer that way."

It was a warning that was all too necessary, especially for Mark.

When Sid, Nick, and I got home, Sid presented me with my term paper, all typed and with the footnotes in the body.

"Honey, thank you. I mean, I could have done this."

"Nah. I had some time tonight, and it would have taken you all day to do it. It didn't take me any time at all." Sid is a good and fast typist. "Besides, I'm a teacher now. I frown on students ditching class."

Friday, Richard the Third opened. Nick was in the men's dressing room, but I found out that several helium-filled balloons had landed next to his makeup station. There was a vase of mixed flowers next to mine, with a note.

"Break a leg," it read in Sid's atrocious, cramped handwriting. "Just please do it carefully."

I remembered to put my wedding rings in my wallet and didn't forget again. Nick had been climbing up and down the walls all day, first at school, then at home through dinner. Neither of us could eat much. It would have been nice to have had a little bit of peace getting our makeup on, but Lindsey had brought her boom box in, as usual. We'd all been singing along to Billy Joel's The Nylon Curtain album during tech.

Terry had gotten in early and had done the entire play on the stage. Dr. Dorfmann gathered us all backstage for a quick pep talk. I winked at Frank, who was up on a catwalk above the stage with the other musicians. The dancers in steel gray leotards and hoods slid into place, some wearing tabards with white roses on them, some with the boar representing Richard. Terry bounced silently up and down, shaking his hands. His costume was the same medieval tunic and tights all the men were wearing, but it was black, and there was the hump centered on his back and trailing tendrils of fabric from his arms. Dom was over in another corner of the backstage area, doing stretches. Several of us went back to the green room. Nick curled up on one of the couches with his knitting and his book. He had a good chunk of the play to get through before his first scene came up. Tyler hung close to his mother and ignored everyone else. I couldn't help thinking that he was going to be just like Kaspar when he grew up. Both boys were wearing white tunics and tights with the same red fox fake-fur that my costume had.

We could hear the audience rumbling from the house. I knew Sid was there, somewhere. I took a few deep breaths. Yeah, I was nervous, which was okay. You're supposed to be a little nervous. I'd played many a role before while working with Sid. The nice thing about this role was that I had a fancy costume, and no one would likely be shooting at me.

Then the audience hushed, the music began, and a moment later…

"Now is the winter of our discontent made glorious summer by this son of York…" Terry began.

There is something about opening night. Everybody was on. There were a couple mishaps. One of the dancers had her tabard get caught on the bier with Henry VI (supposedly) on it. I cried as the dancer soldiers surrounded Nick and Tyler and danced them away, and almost got mascara down my cheek. Dom almost gagged during the dance when Clarence got dumped into the butt of malmsey. It was sort of mimed, with some dancers helping the murderer (Mark Debich), and some forming the infamous barrel of wine, with lighting adding the color, instead of anything on stage.

In fact, the set was largely bare, but painted the same gray as the English sky so frequently was. Richard had a set piece that he climbed on and off, and it vaguely resembled a web. But almost any effect and color were from the lights and nothing else.

The fun part was the ghosts cursing Richard and blessing Richmond, also played by Dominic. It was one of the rare moments Terry was not on stage, and as the rest of us gathered to get ready for the curtain call, I could see him breathing heavily and shaking his hands out again. A black curtain had been pulled down across the back of the stage as Richmond and Richard went to their respective tents. Dom slid quickly out of his tent and swapped wigs in an instant, almost getting the Clarence wig on crooked. Katie set it straight. Then the ghosts appeared and disappeared. All you saw were their faces, including Nick's and Tyler's as the murdered princes, and all they had were lights, but the way the lights blinked on and off, it looked like heads bobbing back and forth as they did their thing. Then the curtain dropped to the stage floor (on purpose).

The final battle scene was danced, another reason why Dominic had been cast as both Clarence and Richmond. Terry moved through it nicely - dance was one of the required classes for all students.

Then it was over. The stage went dark and when the lights came up again, the dancers were in place, the musicians among them. The rest of the cast walked on, mostly in groups. Nick and Tyler took their bow together and my heart swelled with pride when the cheers rose in volume for them. [You got a good swell in cheering, too, and deserved it. - SEH] Then Terry took his bow and got a standing ovation. There was one final bow, and then the lights went out, we ran offstage, and the house lights went on.

As we filed into the dressing rooms, Tracy Schultz got on the loudspeaker and called out the names of everyone expected to show at the faculty reception, although the whole cast was invited. I was one of the ones expected to show. Nick wasn't, but he would be there, anyway. Tyler's mother took him home early.

The only thing that marred the whole night was the ongoing anger at Kaspar's interruption at the rehearsal on Wednesday. There were considerable cheers telling Kaspar to do something obscene to himself as we changed out of our costumes, got them checked in, then washed up. Sid had asked me to wear my cashmere dress to the reception, so I did, happily. The reward would be worth it and then some.

At the reception, some of the faculty asked me about what had happened with Kaspar and I simply replied that I didn't know. I had thought of a good reason why he was a bit of a mess. If he cared as deeply about his finishing students as Noah Taplin had implied, then he was probably feeling pretty sad and couldn't talk about it with anybody, because no one was supposed to know that he had a connection with them.

I held my breath as Raylene and Mimi simpered their way up to me.

"I must say, Linda," Raylene said. "You are quite the actress."

I smiled. "Thank you, Raylene. I haven't acted since high school, but it's been fun taking it up again."

"And your son did a lovely job, too." Mimi said without an ounce of sincerity.

"I'm so proud of him." I gave her a look and left it at that.

The only thing that worried me that night was that Nick, Terry, Dom, and Mark spent some significant time together. There was definitely something up. I debated calling them on it, but I had no real reason to. Just suspicion.

Oh, and the cashmere dress had the desired effect on Sid. It was a really good night all around.

March 18 – 21, 1987

One nice thing about Richard being in performance was that Nick and I had Monday through Thursday nights off. Which was a good thing that first Monday night. When Sid had gotten our mail from back home on Sunday, there were three letters addressed to me. I had sent out the three applications for PhD programs in English Literature the fall before. I'd been so tired the night before, Sid hadn't given them to me. But at dinner, Sid placed them next to my plate.

"They're all pretty thick," I said. "That's a good sign."

"Well, are you going to open them?" Nick asked.

I did. I'd been accepted at my preferred two universities and put on the waiting list at the one I was not as excited about.

"Wow," I said, shaking. "I'm really going to do this finally."

Sid pulled me up and hugged me, then Nick slammed into both of us.

"I'm so proud of you," said Nick.

"I am, too," said Sid. "Congratulations, sweetheart."

I looked at the letters and paperwork. "Now, I just have to choose which one, and it looks like I've got 'til the middle of April to decide where."

The celebration was kept short. I still had some studying to do that night. It was also finals week, well, for those of us studying or working at the university. Nick just had school and insisted on visiting the chem lab after, even though the Lab Rats were supposedly finished for the quarter.

Finals also meant that Sid was up to his ears in exams and term papers to grade, so while I was finally free by Tuesday, he was anything but. I helped with the Western Civ term papers, though.

Outside, it seemed as though the snow had melted overnight. The weather was still a little on the chilly side, but warmer than it had been, and the snow had been melting since the ice storm a week or so before. It was finally spring, and suddenly, people were on the sidewalks, wearing sweaters instead of parkas, coming out to feel the sun on their faces. Trees were budding, and a few flowers poked their way up along the front walk of our house.

Then Clayton Webster was found strangled outside the Performing Arts building on Wednesday.

I don't know why the campus didn't shut down. It would have made sense. But Sebastian Lovegood was determined that life should go on and that the police would capture the Campus Killer in no time. Irene was in Randall's lab when I went to pick Nick up that afternoon, and both Irene and I were annoyed.

"I think the only reason I'm not up in arms is that I know he only has one more potential victim," Irene said.

"Two more, if you count Kaspar," I said. "But I could almost cheer the killer on for that one."

Irene laughed. "I heard. Good lord, what was that about?"

"Honestly?" I shrugged. "I suspect he's grieving and worrying about getting killed. Not to mention worrying about what his bosses will do. The finishing school is supposedly a plum position."

"Still, I have a couple students in that cast. They were really pissed off."

"They're all furious." I looked over at Nick. "I've got a feeling there is some form of revenge being planned, never mind that the reviews have been overwhelmingly positive."

"Well, we're going to see the show on Sunday."

"Great. I hope you enjoy it."

Irene laughed. "I don't know. Randall is not exactly a fan of Shakespeare. On the other hand, he is a big fan of Ryan's. I have to say, he has gotten such a kick out of your kid."

"Good." I beamed. "It's really hard not to, but I'm a little on the biased side."

Irene blinked and giggled. "You are so lucky to have him."

"I am," I said, my eyes filling.

I was insanely lucky to have Nick.

We got home and Nick took one look at Sid and ran for his bedroom. Sid was dusting in the living room.

"Why are you doing that?" I asked, and none too gently.

"Because you forgot to do it yesterday. Again."

"I've been a little busy."

"Really? You've had nights off this week. Your term paper is done, with help from me, may I remind you. The only final you have left is your meeting with Kaspar. So, please explain to me how it is that you can't remember a basic chore that you remembered while working on a term paper during tech week!"

I folded my arms across my chest. "You could have just reminded me. You usually do."

Sid threw the dusting rag onto the coffee table. "I have been working my ass off, grading exams and term papers. I do the all the cooking. Is it so much to ask that you stay on top of the chores you agreed to?"

"I am helping you with the term papers. In fact, that's probably why I forgot to dust last night. I know you told me not to worry about it on Monday. So why are you up in arms now? Could it be it's not the dusting?"

"Keeping this place clean is important, and it is not going to happen unless we stay on top of it. Which means we can't just forget to do things."

"I agree and I have done my chores, even a few times when I was dead tired. So, we worked on the term papers last night. You could have just waited until I got home and asked me when I was going to dust. You didn't have to just do it and then get mad."

Sid huffed a little. He knew darned well I was right, but wasn't quite ready to acknowledge it.

"What's really going on, honey?" I looked at him, feeling worried.

"We're going to be stuck here another quarter." He sighed and looked up at the ceiling. "The teaching has been fun, but I hate being here. I hate trying to live on an associate's salary. I hate having to do our own housework. And I really hate those assholes I'm working with. Last Friday, I went back and forth about asking you to wear the cashmere to the reception, but I thought, what the hell. We both love how that dress turns me on. We deserve that kind of treat. Why not? But then there's Weber, who pretended he was joking, then said if it hadn't been for you and that dress, he might still be married."

"Which is nonsense. His wife had already kicked him out once last November."

"I know!" Sid started pacing. "But Horton and Westin are also giving me grief because all of a sudden, their wives want to scream during sex like you do, and I'm, like, guys, with your attitudes, I'm surprised you get sex at all. And some of the other guys around campus are getting crap from their wives about me supporting you taking classes, about me kissing you in public. Like it's that hard to be nice to someone you love? What is wrong with these people?"

"I haven't the faintest idea." I shrugged. "But then I never have had the faintest idea about things like that. It's one of the reasons you and I have never done well with the other parents at our son's school back home."

Sid winced. "Are they really that neurotic back home?"

"Oh, yes. At least, the women are. The men don't talk to me that much."

Sid frowned as he tried to parse it out. "The guys in the choir at church aren't that bad. But now I have to wonder if that's because their wives are generally there and we're in church when we're practicing."

At home, Sid plays the organ and piano for the Guitar Choir, which is directed by Frank.

"And those folks tend to be a lot more liberal than the people out here." I started pacing. "Although, the liberal folks can get me peeved, too. It's the whole 'I'm right, you're wrong' thing that neither of us likes."

Sid sank onto the couch. "So, how is it that you're on such an even keel right now and I'm going nuts?"

"Oh, come on. You get pretty pissed off when someone dumps that judgmental crap on us, even back home." I shrugged. "As for me, here we're not us, so it can't be about who we really are. That makes it a lot easier to let it roll off my back."

"True. It is a good thing for the case that my contract is for two quarters, but it is not a good thing for my sanity." He looked up at me. "And we have no idea who this killer is. Every last person we could reasonably suspect has been alibied for at least one of the murders, and we know the same person murdered everybody because the marks on their necks match. So, what do we do now?"

"Pray like crazy that Mark Debich doesn't get killed? I really like Mark."

Sid reached over, grabbed my hand, and gently pulled me down next to him on the couch.

"My beloved sweetheart," he whispered, nuzzling my ear. "You would find a way to like Hitler."

I finished the dusting, then called Nick out of his bedroom to help his father and me make dinner.

I spent Thursday helping Sid get caught up on his term papers and exams. And doing some more housework. Both of us worked together on that one because, really, housework sucks.

Friday, I had my one-on-one conference with Earnest Kaspar. I wasn't sure what to expect. The man had not taken any notes during class. I can't say his critiques on my work were totally off-base. Truth be told, he was right more often than not. At least, when he'd deigned to notice that I'd done something. Or was forced to acknowledge I'd done something because I was one of his students. Most of the rest of the time, he'd ignored me.

I noticed that the crack under the door to his office was black when I knocked on the door at the appointed time. A light flipped on, and Kaspar opened the door, greeted me with no interest whatsoever, and admitted me. He seated himself behind his desk. I waited a moment for the invitation to sit down in one of the two chairs in front, then just sat down anyway.

The office was relatively spare. There was a couch, of course, and several putty-colored filing cabinets. But the walls were largely bare except for a huge poster on the side wall next to his desk. It was for a movie called "Light of Day." It looked like a black-and-white photo of a small forest had been overlaid by red. The credits were all underneath the bare trees. I didn't initially look at them too closely.

"Linda Devereaux," Kaspar muttered, then looked intently at me. "Why are you here?"

"I'm doing undergrad prerequisites so that I can get my master's in theatre."

"You don't have any genuine interest in theatre."

"Actually, I do." I looked him in the eye, but then looked down at the side of his desk closest to the back wall. There was an empty vodka bottle in the waste can there.

"You'll never make it in Hollywood," he grumbled, as if that was reason enough to dismiss me.

I glared at him. "I don't want to make it in Hollywood."

His eyes darted to the poster. I looked at it as well. The movie had been directed by Fedor Andreyevich. His real name.

"I want to teach theatre at the high school level," I continued.

His eyebrows rose a fraction of a millimeter. "I suppose. Well." He looked down at the papers on his desk. "You have terrible taste in plays. Your composition is labored. But you know how to work with actors."

"Thanks. I guess." I looked at the poster again. "That must have been an interesting film."

He glared at me. "It is a lost dream, nothing more. We are finished here."

"Okay. Thanks."

I left the office, my mind whirling. I was no longer the least bit concerned about my grade. Evidence? That's what I needed to get.

I hurried up to Sid's office in the Humanities building. He was there, filling out the final grade reports for his students.

"Hey, lover," I said, grinning.

"Hey." He smiled.

I went over to where he was sitting behind his desk and gave him a big, warm kiss.

"Nice," he whispered. "Does this mean we're about to get some?"

"It might. But I thought you'd rather know that we're not going to be here another quarter."

His jaw didn't quite drop, but close enough to dropping to be gratifying.

"I know who the killer is," I said. "At least, I'm pretty sure I do. We just have to figure out how to verify it and, preferably, get him arrested."

Sid pulled me into his lap. "And what did my darling genius uncover?"

"A motive that went past all of us." I kissed him again. "Kaspar may have been promoted to his current position, but I'm willing to bet some serious money that he did not see it as a promotion. I do not know what made him go round the twist. However, he is pretty mad that he didn't get to stay in Hollywood."

Sid thought. "And he's the only one on our suspect list who is not alibied for any of the murders."

"Exactly. He's also been spending a lot of time in his office with the lights off. I saw an empty vodka bottle in his waste can. Admittedly, that's not court-worthy evidence."

"But it's enough to get us looking a lot more closely at him." Sid frowned. "But how do we do that?"

"That we'll have to think about."

"I'm going to take a chance and call the team in on this."

"Nick and I have call at six."

Call meaning the time we had to be at the theater for the performance that night.

"We'll meet at our place tomorrow afternoon. Why not? It's your birthday."

I snorted. "I'm not worried about that."

That night, however, gave us the opening we needed, even as I was about to take my son's head off. Not to mention Dominic's, Terry's, and Mark's heads. I hadn't been mistaken. They had been planning on some revenge. The biggest problem I had was that it would give me exactly the opportunity to search Kaspar's office that we needed.

To Breanna, 8/7/00
Topic of the Day: Things That Went Boom
Hey, Lover -

Um, Mom told you that the big downside of having been in the spy biz, even unofficially, does kind of mean that I'm never completely out of it, right? And that I'm still doing favors for my folks. So, um, well, that big explosion in the supposed tire factory downtown that you think I know more about than I should. Okay. You're right. I know a lot more about it.

It's why I keep my certification in explosives up to date, even though I really shouldn't need it, given my research. My folks almost never call me. But if they need to blow something up, I get the call. You can't blame them. I'm damned good at it. And it is fun. No pun intended, but that supposed tire factory was a blast. It wasn't a tire factory, but a munitions dump for a radical group that was getting ready to blow up innocent people. The explosion gave the ATF agents the excuse they needed to go in, and they got the evidence they needed to arrest the idiots.

I got my start on the Kansas case. I've told you about some of it. The blast was one of the high points, and that whole case was a lot of fun. We'd been planning it since the show opened, these guys, Terry, Dominic, Mark, and me. We were so mad at Professor Kaspar. It was Dominic's idea to go in and plant the stink bomb. We just had to figure out how to get the door open. I thought about it and knew I could assemble the right chemicals. Whether they'd blow the lock open, I didn't know. But Terry said even blowing up the door would be a good start. And I admit, I had help.

I shouldn't have been supporting what the kids had come up with. After all, the older boys had been cheering my son on and encouraging him to come up with one of his more explosive experiments. So, when I overheard them that night during intermission, I was not happy, but at the same time, my head whirled with the possibilities.

That Saturday morning, Frank, Esther, Kathy, Jesse, Irene, and Randall all arrived at our house. Sid outlined the plan. Randall agreed to help Nick put together the right formula. We set things up for just after the show finished. That way, all the costumes would be checked in and the building almost deserted. I would have suggested early that next morning, but Dom, Terry, and Mark would never have gone for it.

Nick's job was to convince his confederates to do it, which was insanely easy to do, according to Nick. The rest of us would be stationed around the building, wearing our transmitters, just in case Kaspar was in his office with the lights turned out. I must admit, I was pretty tired when I came offstage after the curtain call that night, but there was no help for it. I had to be just close enough to the office to get in after the blast, but not so close that I'd have been able to prevent it.

I put on jeans and an Oxford shirt, and washed my face, even with the earpiece parked on my ear, so small you had to really look to see it. Nick coughed to let me know his transmitter was on.

"Little Red is on," I said, softly.

"Big Red standing by," said Sid's voice.

Frank, Esther, Jesse, and Kathy all checked in. Randall laughed softly. He and Irene were outside the building, acting as lookouts.

"Kaspar is in the theater lobby," Kathy said. "Not sure what he's doing there. He seems to be just standing there."

"Tiny Red," said Sid to Nick. "Start operations now."

Nick coughed again. "Come on, guys. Let's blow the sucker before my mom catches us."

I heard the other guys laugh. I waited a couple minutes, then slid out of the ladies' dressing room. The four of them were headed down the hall to the department offices without looking behind them.

Several minutes later, while I waited around the corner from the offices, I heard a loud bang. Nick yelped in joy.

"It worked!"

"Yee-hah!" cried Dominic. "Let's get that stink bomb set up and get out of here."

"Yeah, but where do we want to put it?" Terry asked.

"I dunno," Dominic said. "Hey, where did Mark go?"

"Let's not worry about that now," said Terry.

"I'm going to search his desk," Dominic said. "Maybe we'll find something." There was the sound of a drawer opening. "Like all these vodka bottles."

"That's a lot of booze," said Nick.

"Come on," said Terry. "Let's get this thing set and go."

Another drawer opened.

"Look at these files." Dominic's voice grew solemn. "Terry, wasn't there, like, a Clayton Webster that got killed this past week?"

"What?" Terry swore loudly. "Those are all the people that the Campus Killer got."

"Then why does each one of these have a big X through the top page and 'Done' written on it?" Dominic sounded scared.

Terry swore again. "Um, Dom. Forget the stink bomb. We need to get out of here. Now."

I rolled around the corner. "Ryan? Are you over here?"

Nick swore. "My mom!"

"Dom, we need to get out of here."

"I'm taking this one. The cops will need to see it."

"What's going on?" I demanded, walking into the office. "How did you guys get in here?"

"Linda, take Ryan," said Terry.

"Hey," said Dominic. "There's a file here on Mark Debich."

"Where is he?" I asked.

Terry looked a little helpless. "He took off for some reason."

"Debich is talking to Kaspar," Kathy said. "They've gone into the school hallway."

I worked on keeping my face blank. "You know, guys, maybe we should look for Mark. That killer got two people within two weeks. He may be escalating."

The guys looked terrified. I grabbed Nick's arm and pulled him out of the office with me. We ran for the front of the building, while the two other guys headed to the back hall.

I looked at Nick. "I think I know where Mark and Kaspar are. I want you to go to the offices, see if you can find a phone and call the cops. Okay?"

"Mom!"

"Do as I tell you. We need cops. Now."

I ran for the stairs next to the costume shop.

"Little Red, where are you?" Sid's voice asked.

"Heading to our favorite rendezvous spot."

A minute later, Sid met me on the stairs to the costume warehouse. I ran ahead and got into the warehouse first. Kaspar had forced Mark to the back of the first aisle and reached for Mark's throat. I screamed as loudly as I could.

Kaspar turned and ran straight at me, knocking me aside, then Sid, as well.

"Subject is headed for the back stairs, toward the back of the theatre," Sid's voice said.

I ran over to Mark. "Are you alright?"

He nodded. "I'm okay. How did you get here?"

"Long story. I've got to get Kaspar. He's the Campus Killer."

Mark gulped. "I think I figured that one out."

"Come on."

Sid had already run downstairs. Mark and I ran for the back stairs as well. Somehow, we both ended up in the house of the big main theater. The house lights were up, and the stage sat in shadows. I'm not sure how it had happened, but Kaspar stood about midway up the side aisle, his arm around Kathy's neck and a snub-nosed pistol aimed at her temple. Terry was right in front of the stage, crouching, with a small automatic in one hand. He tossed another to Jesse. Sid was on Terry's other side, his smaller automatic in his hands.

"We've called the police," Sid said. "You can't get away with this."

Kaspar just laughed. Jesse looked a little panicked, then calmed a little as he saw Esther sliding into the house from the lobby. Mark had disappeared again, but Kaspar glanced back at me as I came into the house and dismissed me. I dove down between the seats nearest me and started inching my way forward.

"You touch a hair on her head, and I swear you will die," Jesse said. Frank wandered in from the wings, then stood stock still.

"I no longer care," Kaspar said. "They ruined my life. They took away my dream. What have I got to live for?"

As I inched forward, I couldn't help grinning and thanked God for another miracle. Dom's missing ball of yarn and needle sat underneath the aisle seat one row below me. I inched forward and reached, just barely getting it.

Kaspar backed up the aisle. "I'm leaving here. I don't care anymore."

I grabbed the needle. As the back of Kaspar's knee reached me, I jabbed as hard as I could. Kaspar bent in pain, and that gave Kathy just what she needed. She knocked the gun out of his hand, then whipped around and punched him in the gut, and then the side of his head.

That's when the police showed. They saw Jesse with a gun and aimed at him, but Terry yelled at them.

"He's not the bad guy!" Terry started up the aisle and pretty much put himself between the two officers and Jesse. He also cursed a lot. "This idiot on the floor is. He's the Campus Killer. You leave my friend over here alone. He was just trying to protect his wife."

I'd had no idea that Terry and Jesse had gotten that friendly, but I was glad. We were all exhausted by the time the detectives arrived. Dom gave them the file he had taken from Kaspar's office. We were all interviewed multiple times before we were finally dismissed.

When Sid and I got home, we told Nick how proud we were of him, then sent him to bed. And for the first time in a very long time, Sid and I went to sleep without making love first.

March 22 – 24, 1987

It was bittersweet the night Richard closed. I must admit, the sound of the applause was very gratifying. The cast party afterward was a blast. Sid and I even let Nick attend, although I kept a careful eye on him. There was a lot of booze flowing, and Nick does like wine. He doesn't overindulge, but there was always the chance it would sneak up on him. Fortunately, it didn't.

We never would find out what had set Kaspar off, but he had been determined to wipe out the finishing school. There was a note to that effect in one of the other drawers of his desk. He died the night he was arrested, apparently from some poison.

At the cast party, Mark seemed... Not off, but different.

"You okay?" I asked him.

"I'm fine." He shrugged. "I'm a KGB agent, you know. But I'm defecting. I just did one last job for those SOBs, then the CIA is going to let me do what I really want to do. To write scripts and see them produced."

"That sounds great," I said. "But why are you telling me this?"

"I'm telling everyone." He grinned.

I had a bad feeling he had really wanted me specifically to know.

I said goodbye to everyone, including Dr. Dorfmann, with a small pang, knowing that I would not likely ever see them again. But that was how our business worked.

Sid turned in his resignation Monday morning, then called the movers. We spent the rest of the day packing those items we wanted to take home and getting them shipped. The rest of the stuff in the house would be donated to charity when the movers came the next morning.

Raylene came by that afternoon, utterly indignant. "You're leaving us?"

"I'm afraid so," I said. "Charles got offered a tenure track position back in California, and that's where we really want to be. I should even be able to get my old teaching job back."

"You know, Carl was going to offer to make his position here permanent."

"I'm glad Carl thought so highly of him." I smiled at her, this time genuinely. "It was nice knowing you, Raylene."

"Nice knowing you, Linda." She sighed and walked back to her house.

Mimi did not come to say goodbye. When I went to the test school the next morning to formally un-enroll Nick, Ms. Westmore told me that Jimmy Deering had not only gotten in trouble again, he had gotten beyond the attempt and had raped another young woman. [I was glad that Irene kept track of them. Fortunately, Jimmy was tried as an adult and did some jail time, and I've heard here and there that he's been in and out of jail on rape charges. - SEH]

Irene and Randall showed slightly after the movers did to drive us to Kansas City and the airport. They also had news.

"We're coming out of hiding," Irene said. "We get to have our old names back and we've got posts at Northwestern University. Randall, I mean, Max, even found a way so that the work we published while we were here would be credited to us, which means we're that much closer to tenure at NU."

"Oh, I'm so happy for you!" Grinning, I gave her a big hug.

The first call for boarding on the flight to Los Angeles rang out over the loudspeaker. Irene sighed.

"Does this mean we're not going to see you again?"

I smiled softly. "I'm afraid so." I slipped a small piece of paper into her hand. "But Sid Hackbirn, Lisa Wycherly, and Nick Flaherty would love to hear from you when you get settled. Keep you on the Christmas card list and all that."

Irene laughed and hugged me solidly. Nick was a little teary-eyed as he hugged Randall, but then the three of us got on the plane and headed for home.

April 15, 1987

It figures it had to happen during Holy Week. That's the week immediately before Easter and it's a big deal in the Catholic church. Sid, Nick, and I had been back for almost a month. We'd fallen back into our usual routines quickly. Motley, my springer spaniel, was a little needy for a while. Nick took the dog with him to go skateboarding several afternoons after school, and that helped. The cats, well, they were cats. Long John Silver let Sid know she was not happy to have been deprived of his lap, her favorite napping spot, for so long. Her two grown offspring didn't seem to care that we'd returned, except for the one who pooped in one of Sid's dress shoes. We still don't know which one does that.

I'd gotten Nick permission to knit at school, but he decided he didn't want to chance the other boys making fun of him, and I couldn't blame him. So, he was bored, and the only thing that made it better was that he'd been accepted at a Jesuit high school for boys and that both his cousin Darby O'Malley and his best friend Josh Sandoval would be going with him. The school was known for its challenging curriculum. Nick would also be eligible for Advanced Placement classes and would get to take classes at the local community college at the same time.

I made my final decision about where I was going to do my PhD work and sent in the confirmation just in time.

Frank and Esther returned a week after we did. Esther had decided that she didn't need a master's degree to start a company, at least not one in engineering. She was debating about an MBA, though. Frank immediately applied at the same school where Sid was finishing his master's degree and a couple other places. Only Frank wanted to major in choral music. Or liturgical music. He hadn't made up his mind.

I'm not sure when Kathy and Jesse got back to Los Angeles, but the six of us and Nick went to dinner on Palm Sunday and Kathy's pregnancy was definitely showing. Jesse had an impressive collection of photos, and the show will be later this summer. Kathy was thrilled to have missed tax season. She's an accountant, but was seriously considering putting that aside to become a full-time mom.

April tenth, Sid and I celebrated the day we first made our promises to each other to spend the rest of our lives together and to be faithful. That was our couple day, and it was lovely.

Wednesday of Holy Week, I'd had to stop by the rectory office at church to pick up the Eucharistic Minister schedule and work out a couple last second details for the Triduum, which are the three main services for Easter, namely Holy Thursday, Good Friday, and the Easter Vigil that Saturday night. There are also the masses on Easter Sunday, but I wasn't involved with those.

Margaret Dyson was in the office, too, that day. She was on the Liturgy Committee. I had joined the previous fall when I'd given up going to the Tuesday night bible study. I was still banned from the Teen Bible Study on Mondays because I have a teen. As for the Liturgy Committee, Margaret was very locked into doing things the way they'd always been done and had seen me as an obstacle. I was sure she'd been ecstatic when I'd had to take off right after Christmas.

"Oh, Lisa." She smiled and came up to me. "How are you?"

"Doing well. You?"

"Fine. Just fine." She paused. "Um, Lisa, I don't know how to say this. But there are a couple people on the Liturgy Committee who find you, well, a little forceful."

"Oh. Who?"

She smiled. "I was asked not to say. No one wants to hurt your feelings."

"Oh, Margaret," I sighed. "I'm so sorry they feel intimidated by me. I can't imagine why anyone would feel that way. Worse yet, who wouldn't want to work things out up front, instead of hiding and spreading distrust among the committee members? You guys are nicer than that." Okay, Margaret wasn't, but I was purposely laying it on a bit thick. "Margaret, darling, if you hear people complaining about me, would you please tell them to speak to me directly and we'll work it out? I'm not an ogre and I don't bite. I'd hate for people to be afraid of me simply because they don't know me. I can trust you to do that, can't I?"

Margaret couldn't answer, so I smiled.

"I've got to go meet my husband," I said. "If you'll excuse me?"

I told Sid about it that night as we got ready for bed.

"It's just annoying that she's being so petty," I grumbled as I rinsed my toothbrush.

Sid finished rinsing his contact lenses. Both his and Nick's hair had been restored to their natural color, as had mine. Nick threw away his contact lenses. Sid wanted to throw away his glasses, but he occasionally needed them.

"That's normal for that crowd," he said. "At least you're not all upset that someone is mad at you."

I shrugged. "It's their problem. I'm tired of worrying about it."

Sid pulled me close to him and kissed my temple. "That's more like the woman I know." He smiled. "You're different since we got back from Kansas. More like your old self."

"I suppose."

We walked over to our bed and got under the sheets. Sid slid over and snuggled next to me.

"Actually, I think you've been more like your old pre-married self since before we got back," he said. "You've even been calling me your husband rather than your spouse."

"You're right." I thought about it. "Huh. I think I finally know what happened to me. It's what I said in Kansas about the faculty wives' and your colleagues' BS not being about us because we weren't us. Only in a way, we were. But, yeah, the whole losing myself thing started when you and I became a couple that year before we got married. Before then, it was just me, and if some people got judgmental, I didn't care because they didn't know me. I didn't like it, but it was no big deal. Then you and I made our lifetime promises to each other, and you became a part of me. So, when someone questioned our choices, it wasn't just judging me, it was judging you, too. Then Nick became a part of us, and it was judging him. I started feeling like I had to defend us, because it wasn't just me, anymore, it was you guys, as well. Worse yet, being so afraid of losing myself in the relationship, I began to think I had."

"But you really hadn't." Sid looked at me. "Even as worried as you were, I could see that you were still there."

"That's probably why I was so confused. I hadn't lost myself. I was still the woman who really didn't care about what others thought of her choices. But then we went to Kansas and there were all these people trying to judge all three of us who had no idea that we were not the people they thought we were. And it really didn't make a darned bit of difference what they thought. When Margaret started her game today, I realized she and her anonymous friends don't have the first clue about who we are, and probably never will. It's annoying, of course, because of having to dance around their BS. We both know confronting them with it will never work. But it really has nothing to do with any of the three of us. It's about them and their limitations and if they can't get past that, well, fuck them."

Sid's jaw dropped, and he laughed. "Did I just hear you say that?"

"It's the vilest word I can think of, and it's vile behavior." I nuzzled him. "The bottom line is that I didn't lose me by getting married. The risk was there, without question. I did have everything to lose. But I also had everything to gain, and I did. I'm still who I've always been. I'm just growing, is all. I have you as part of me. I have Nick as part of me, and the people we love. But I'm still there, too." I chuckled. "It's ironic as hell that it took pretending to be someone else to get me to see that I was still who I am."

Sid gently grasped my chin. "Who you are is the woman I love so very, very much. And you and Nick are so much a part of me now that I do not know if I would recognize myself without you."

"I love you, Sid. I love being with you. I love when we're working together. And I love being who I am with you."

Sid laughed gently and then got frisky. It was delicious. Best of all, it was real.

Coming Soon

PATHS NOT TAKEN is book thirteen in the Operation Quickline series.

There's still time to change the road you're on

When the head of Operation Quickline, the ultra-secret organization that Lisa Wycherly and Sid Hackbirn work for, sets up a sting at the resort belonging to Lisa's parents, Lisa and Sid are fit to be tied. But telling Dale O'Connor no is not possible.

Summer hire Dusty Simpson is the target, and Sid and Lisa reluctantly take on surveilling him while working the same jobs they had as teens. Sid's working the restaurant at Wycherly's Family Resort. Lisa is head of housekeeping. Even their son Nick is hired to bus tables.

But then an old nemesis shows up, and the sting turns out to be nothing like what Sid and Lisa thought. The nemesis is killed and it looks like a trap was set for Dusty. Not to mention that a computer disk with critical data has disappeared.

With Lisa's academic career in a questionable state, Nick sulking because he can't go to science camp, and clashes among the resort staff, Lisa has enough to keep her hands full. If only she can keep her father from figuring out about her secret double life.

Thank You for Reading

I do hope you enjoyed the book.

If you can do me one small favor, please. Can you go to one of the social media/retail profiles below and leave a short review? It doesn't need to be a lot, just honest.

Other books by Anne Louise Bannon

I'm so glad you liked this book! Check out my other novels, available in print or ebook at your favorite retailer:

Old Los Angeles Series:

Death of the Zanjero

Death of the City Marshal

Death of the Chinese Field Hands

Death of an Heiress

Death of the Drunkard

Operation Quickline Series:

That Old Cloak and Dagger Routine

Stopleak

Deceptive Appearances

Fugue in a Minor Key

Sad Lisa

These Hallowed Halls

My Sweet Lisa

A Little Family Business

Just Because You're Paranoid

From This Day Forward

Silence in the Tortured Soul

Amateur Theatricals

Freddie and Kathy Series:

Fascinating Rhythm

Bring Into Bondage

The Last Witnesses

Blood Red

Daria Barnes:

Rage Issues

Mrs. Sperling:

A Nose for a Niedeman

Brenda Finnegan:

Tyger, Tyger

Romantic Fiction:

White House Rhapsody, Book One and Two

Fantasy and Science Fiction:

A Ring for a Second Chance

But World Enough and Time

Time Enough

And I would be honored if you left a review for this and any of my books on the below sites. It really helps.

- bookbub.com/profile/anne-louise-bannon
- goodreads.com/author/show/513383.Anne_Louise_Bannon
- facebook.com/RobinGoodfellowEnt/

twitter.com/ALBannon

amazon.com/stores/author/B00JCRXST2?ingress=0&visitId=bfadb491-d1ac-4575-84da-bb4f7d325ad9&store_ref=ap_rdr&ref_=ap_rdr

Connect with Anne Louise Bannon

Thank you for sticking it out this long! Please join my newsletter. It's the best way to stay up-to-date on my upcoming projects, blog posts and even the occasional game and giveaway.

You can sign up for my newsletter on Substack, Substack.com/@annelouisebannon. or by visiting my website, annelouisebannon.com

And don't forget to connect with me on your favorite social media platforms:

- bookbub.com/profile/anne-louise-bannon
- goodreads.com/author/show/513383.Anne_Louise_Bannon
- facebook.com/RobinGoodfellowEnt/
- amazon.com/stores/author/B00JCRXST2?ingress=0&visitId=bfadb491-d1ac-4575-84da-bb4f7d325ad9&store_ref=ap_rdr&ref_=ap_rdr
- pinterest.com/AnneLouiseBannon
- instagram.com/annelouisebannon4/

About Anne Louise Bannon

Anne Louise Bannon is an author and journalist who wrote her first novel at age 15. Her journalistic work has appeared in Ladies' Home Journal, the Los Angeles Times, Wines and Vines, and in newspapers across the country. She was a TV critic for over 10 years, founded the YourFamilyViewer blog, and created the OddBallGrape.com wine education blog with her husband, Michael Holland. She is the co-author of Howdunit: Book of Poisons, with Serita Stevens, as well as author of the Freddie and Kathy mystery series, set in the 1920s, the Old Los Angeles series, set in 1870, and the Operation Quickline series, plus several stand alones. She and her husband live in Southern California with an assortment of critters.

Milton Keynes UK
Ingram Content Group UK Ltd.
UKHW020102050824
446426UK00013B/261